KYLIE KOEWS

Print ISBN: 978-1-916743-01-4
E-Book ISBN: 978-1-916743-00-7

Book Cover by Arina Herman (@arinadrawings) and Gene Levi Chan (@genelevichan.art)
Edited by Jeffery Howe
Formatted by Lina Wesson

First edition 2023 by Burn Books

About the Author

KYLIE KOEWS has been an imaginative and expressive storyteller since she could form complete sentences. She writes stories with strong and relatable heroines and swoon-worthy heroes, offering doses of reality, emotional turmoil, and, most importantly, a lot of love. Currently residing in Portugal, you can find Kylie writing under the shade of the lemon trees in her garden while sipping coffee. *FOREVER YOURS* is her debut novel.

Connect with the author:

Instagram: *@kylie_writes*

Website: www.kyliekoews.com

To Lina,

who was the first person to tell me this should be a book.

1

A Familiar Face

Ten years ago...

THERE'S A PRICE TO PAY for wanting something too much, but Chase Kennedy, eighteen years old and just starting to live his life, was only half aware of this. Standing beneath the string of lights he'd carefully arranged over the cobblestone path in the backyard of his childhood home, he ran his hands through his thick, black hair for the umpteenth time, disregarding the fretful hour he'd spent styling it for this evening.

You can do this, he thought to himself, willing his heartbeat to steady as he wiped his clammy palms against his gray slacks. Deciding the collar of his white button-up was too tight, he clumsily undid the first two buttons.

The night air is a mix of pine from the forest just beyond the backyard and roses he's picked for *her.* As he waited for her

1

arrival, giddy from the recklessness of his proposal, his focus was on the future he'd created inside his head.

"Chase?" A whisper. He turns to see his beloved.

"You look so beautiful." And she did. Her long chestnut hair is styled in soft waves that fall down her back, and she wore a pale pink dress that clung firmly to her tall frame. Of course, they were both young and new to the world, but Chase knew there would never be another woman quite as beautiful as her.

Gently, he wrapped his fingers around her arm and guided her through the path to where he set the table with roses and dinner. She gasps and hooks one slender finger around the delicate, gold heart-shaped pendant on her neck.

"Chase." Another whisper. She seemed confused, almost flustered by his movements.

For a split second, Chase thought about giving up and calling this an innocent dinner to celebrate their second year together, nothing more. But he gave up this idea as soon as it came to him, so blinded was he by the image of her dressed in white.

Before she had the chance to commend the table set up, from the expensive dishware that his mother only used for special occasions and the polaroid pictures of the past year together displayed on twine, to the candles burning vividly and the string lights as bright as the summer sun, he kneels before her.

"Willow Harris," he said.

She held her breath, waiting, disbelieving.

"Will you marry me?"

There was an expectation in his eyes, a display of love that she didn't quite understand yet. When Willow looked at him, she saw herself in his eyes, except it was a version of herself she wanted to be rid of. She was terrified of the mounting pressure the question provoked in her, frightened that she was about to hurt both of them with the answer threatening to burst out of her. But his eyes... they clung to hers.

"Chase..." her hand drifted away from the pendant, and she took a step back. She shivered, not from the chill of the night air but from the question, the expectation, the aching need in his eyes. But she did not want this. "I can't."

Slowly, his smile began to drop, and the green of his eyes seemed to oxidize, turning into the color of rust. He seemed oddly different once she issued her rejection. Willow's heart broke right along with his, but the more she thought about it, the more certain she was of her answer.

"I can't marry you," she said again.

Time slowed to a crawl when the ring slipped out of his hands. Only when it landed at her feet did Willowe notice it.

"Come again?" There's a slight tremor on his lips, and with his knee still pressed against the flattened grass. He shook his head, and she could see the disappointment in his eyes, those eyes which had held *so much* hope just moments before.

When he rose to his feet, she took another step back. Instinctively she raised a hand above her head and twirled it in a circle, like she always did when she was nervous or upset. His eyes followed the pattern numbly, and when she whispered an apology, he swallowed hard and drifted closer.

"Willow, please—"

She shook her head vigorously, and when he reached out for her and she pulled away, he knew it was the end. The candle still burned, and the light from the silvery moon traced a circle on the table, but it was her face, detached and impenetrable, that burned within him. Chase realized that he could barely breathe, but more than that, it became hard for him to turn away from her.

"Why?" he asked, as if it would make any difference.

She simply shook her head again and began to turn away.

Chase knew there were no rules when it came to the endings of relationships, but he also knew that if he didn't act now, he might lose her forever.

"Willow—don't do this."

He wanted her desperately, but she seemed to be pulling further away from him the more he tried to hold on to her.

"I'm sorry," Willow whispered. She wasn't crying, but the tears that threatened to fall surely would if she stayed.

So instead, she ran away from the light and away from his reach while he tried to make sense of this total rejection. There was no added explanation from her before she dashed off, and once she'd left, Chase began to feel an ache like a hole deep in his chest.

"Why?" he asked, even though he knew there would be no answer, even though he knew he was alone again.

The night air was cold and sharp by the time the last candle blew out, and he turned off the lights. In the solitary darkness, Chase stopped breathing.

Ten years later...

Willow has been here before, but it feels new, traipsing through the luxurious foyer of the Wright Hotel with her best friend, Lina, behind her. The wheels of their luggage make light tapping noises as they roll along the marble floor of the foyer, but Willow isn't worried about this. The conversation they've been having is starting to leave a sour taste on the tip of her tongue.

"I'm just saying," Lina says as they move past a group of tourists in matching bright yellow bucket hats congregating near the entrance, seemingly unable to decide where they should be going.

Willow groans, her breathing heavy. "And I'm telling you to drop it."

For a moment, Lina does not press her to speak. The silence is heavy, though it doesn't descend into awkwardness. Years of being absolute best friends allowed for this easy intimacy. But as they walk toward the lobby, Lina starts again with the same fervor almost as though she hadn't stopped in the first place.

"Oh, come on, Willow," she says, her smile wide, vivid, and sincere. "We're in London for crying out loud! And I swear this is the birthplace of the world's sexiest accent spoken by the mouths of the world's sexiest men."

Willow smiles despite herself and hooks a ringed finger around the gold, heart-shaped pendant around her neck. Her face is flushed with exhaustion, but somehow, this turn in the conversation makes her want to laugh.

Lina doesn't mind Willow's humor. She fancies it, in fact, and continues regardless. "Who knows, your future husband could be in the city right now."

"And let me guess…he is one hell of a ghoulishly hand-some devil." Willow lays out her words like bait to trap Lina, but Lina is used to this. She jumps right over it.

"I'm making it my mission to find him!"

Willow tries her hand as well. "I doubt it, but maybe we could find yours."

"Love the sarcasm, but I'm not looking for a husband," she says, and Willow throws her head back, laughing obnoxious-ly.

"What a coincidence." Willow turns away from the name-less faces surrounding them and inclines her head so she can see Lina clearly. "Because neither am I."

Willow begins to laugh as Lina rolls her eyes. Edging closer, she says, "I'll find a man that'll meet your impossibly high standards, Willow Harris."

The bright lights cast a warm, welcoming glow across the lobby of the Wright Hotel. This, coupled with the exhaustion of travel and the relief of arriving, overwhelms Willow in a pleasant rush of endorphins and oxytocin that breaks through her self-imposed walls. She turns slightly toward Lina.

"Perhaps there will be time for that conversation," she says. "In the meantime, how about you find our room keys?"

Lina says, "Oh, really?" while laughing at her friend's diplo-matic attempt to change the subject. "Yeah, yeah, Willow."

Though she's standing in the hotel lobby, and she can see Lina from the corner of her eye, Willow imagines for a moment, just for fun, that she's alone on a brightened pathway, serenely at peace..

She scans the lobby, looking for no one in particular, and shakes her head. Willow runs the fingers of her shaky hand through her hair and licks her lips, nervous. It isn't as though she has an impossibly high standard to meet. It's how she has held on to love's capable of breaking anyone. She knows from experience how tedious it can be to fall in love with just anyone.

For a brief moment, she thinks of *him* again. It's a conflict of choices, a past memory programmed to play inside her head for those times when the loneliness seeps in. And when it does, she shakes it off.

Now is not the time to dwell on the past, she decides.

Willow carefully threads her way across the crowded lobby and heads over to meet Lina at the concierge desk.

It's easy to forget the hushed conversations of the people around her once she's back with Lina, and at the desk, she doesn't mind the heavy footsteps coming from behind them or the barely audible conversations blending together. Whoever they are, they are too far away for her to keep track, but, somehow, as Willow considers them, a familiar melancholy washes over her.

"Are you sure you wouldn't be more comfortable at our house, son?" A man. Willow smiles.

"Lord knows we have the room," a woman's voice curls around Willow's throat, and she begins to turn around.

Lina presses her hands against Willow's. "Keep your focus," she whispers.

"I appreciate the offer, but I have a lot of business here in the city," another man says. "This is more convenient for me."

"Besides, Daddy, our hotels are the best of the best." The new voice is closer; it's a sultry, accented alto. "He'll be more than comfortable."

"You can't argue with that, Bart," the first woman says with a chuckle.

"No, I guess not." A phone chimes and interrupts the moment. "Well, the driver is ready, ladies. We'll see you on Tuesday, son."

And Willow stops listening to the conversation.

Nearby, once the older couple has left, the man takes the woman by the wrist and leads her to the front corner across the

9

lobby. There's an aura of awkwardness that surrounds them as he shifts from one foot to the other, running his hand through his thick, dark hair, and she glances at her manicured fingernails.

"Charlotte," he whispers. His eyes search hers for an answer, but they contain none that he can see. Instead, her gaze holds something he can't define, something that might be occupying a space in her mind where he isn't—but should be.

Chase remembers how their rushed relationship has been and how it's come down to this point in the lobby where the marriage plans hover amidst the ambient hum of the lobby.

Charlotte reaches forward and trails a finger along the length of his arm. She smiles back and presses her hands against her white knitted skirt. She's always wearing something white. At first, Chase thought it was because she was an angel. But now, he's not so sure.

"I'll miss you," Charlotte says coyly.

He sighs and shakes his head. "You can quit the act now, Char; they're gone."

He catches a hint of barely suppressed mirth on her face, but he has nothing to say.

"I can't wish my *fiancé* well before I leave?" She drags the words out quietly as if she knows it might annoy him. "Are you planning to come with me to meet the wedding planner tomorrow?"

Chase crosses his arms and glances past her shoulders to the lighting. He isn't looking at her when he speaks next. "Don't you think we should sit down and talk before we go through with the planning?"

Charlotte drifts closer and lowers her eyes. "There's nothing to talk about, Chase."

"I beg to differ," he swallows, interlocking his fingers behind his neck, gently cradling his head. "We've hardly spoken since my last visit, Char. That's not normal for an engaged couple."

She shakes her head. "I don't know what you're talking about, darling."

Chase calls her bluff. "I'm talking about your distance, Charlotte."

She reaches forward and kisses his cheeks. Chase doesn't pull back but doesn't like how detached she seems or the feelings that run through him at the mere mention of her name.

"You're overthinking again, Chase," she says. "So that's a no to the meeting tomorrow?"

He doesn't hesitate. "I'm meeting with the Williams tomorrow morning, Char, so I won't make it. Are we still on for dinner, though?"

She's already pulling away like he knows she will. "Unless something more important comes up, we are."

"More important than quality time with your fiancé?" He shuffles his feet, and she cups her cheeks. "Let me know."

"Mhmm, listen, darling, I need to go," she whispers. "Call me tomorrow, and we'll discuss dinner."

"Alright."

She flips her hair over her shoulders. As the sunlight glints off of her auburn tresses, Chase catches their fiery brilliance. She's already gone before he even has time to sigh. For years, he's held onto the idea of keeping his distance as a mantra for how to live his life, but with Charlotte, he finds that he has no energy left to keep trying.

Turning back to the lobby, Chase takes in his surroundings. There are people here who he thinks that, perhaps like him, have lives they can barely hang on to. Sometimes, for some of them, maybe it feels like growing pains; but each person has their own stories and private struggles.

When he sees her, Chase thinks he might be dreaming. He's had dreams like this before, where she appears like a fleck of dust caught in the light, visible just out his peripheral vision, something he might soon forget. But this dream's vivid and enticing, drawing him closer as if he was tethered to the end of a string. At once, everything falls apart, and *she* is the only person in this space with him. Long legs in patterned slacks, her fur coat protecting her from the dreary London weather, but it's her hair, locks as dark as his morning coffee, which causes his breath to catch in his throat.

Is that…

It feels too surreal to believe that the woman in front of him is Willow, so he shakes his head and leaves the lobby, exhausted.

As he steps into the elevator, he digs his hands into his hair. His mental exhaustion has his thoughts wandering to places he'd shut out years ago. The slow deterioration of his relationship with Charlotte has only increased the incessant *what-ifs* that plague his mind.

It's her—the woman who left him hanging ten years ago—he keeps seeing her everywhere, and this continuous torture leaves him reeling. If she'd stayed, Chase wonders what would have happened, but there is, of course, nothing to hold on to.

The doors of the elevator are closing, but an almost familiar voice pulls him from his wandering thoughts. The voice is velvety and high-pitched and so dangerously familiar. He holds his breath.

"Wait!" she says. "Hold the elevator!"

Someone else draws closer. "Yeah, that's real classy, Willow."

Chase pauses. Perhaps he is overthinking this, but that name…

Two ladies enter the elevator lobby, and Chase recognizes one of them instantly. It's her.

"Hold the door!" Willow says again and pushes in, with Lina following closely. Then, as she turns to him to thank him, she pauses, startled. The color drains from her face.

"Chase?" she swallows.

Chase's sanity hangs by a tenuous thread when he speaks, disbelief in his tone. "Willow?"

2

Heed the Warning of Stormy Skies

I'M HAVING THAT DREAM AGAIN, aren't I? Chase asks himself. He tugs on the hair at the nape of his neck. *Ouch.* The resulting sharp pain confirms his worst fear. He's awake.

Time moves slowly as he stares at the back of Willow's head. After a decade of waiting, yearning, wishing that she'd walk back into his life, she finally has. But she refuses to look at him.

The woman she stepped into the elevator with glances at him over her shoulder with a curious gaze. She probably has as many questions as Chase does, but he's convinced she'll be the only one to get any answers today.

As much as he wants to speak to Willow, to ask her all the questions that have haunted him for the past ten years, his mouth remains shut. After all, she'd been the one to leave him. Why should he make the first move?

Perhaps she isn't real. Maybe this is a fever dream brought on by exhaustion.

The elevator slows to a stop and the doors open to Willow's floor. Quickly—too quickly, Chase thinks—she takes her exit, followed closely by the woman she entered with. Chase waits momentarily, forcing himself to take slow, steady breaths, thinking she might turn around and acknowledge him.

She doesn't.

Inhale. Exhale.

The doors close, and he's alone once again.

"Willow," he whispers. Her name constricts around his throat so that he can hardly do anything else. For so long, he's asked himself questions. Why did she leave him? Why did she break his heart? Why couldn't she have stayed? Why, why, why? After a while, he resigns himself to the sad reality that he'll probably never hear an answer to any of these questions.

But what about now? He wants answers, of course, but not today. Today, his mind is racing.

"This isn't real," he says. He shoves his hands into his pockets and leans back against the elevator walls. "Out of all the places she could be, why London?"

Once again, Willow crowds his mind and heart, and Chase would only be fooling himself if he claimed not to know why.

His reaction today held enough evidence: a piece of his heart still burns for her.

His first love has walked back into his life like a ghost determined to haunt him. It's a cruel comeback, devastating even for him. Perhaps this is karma; maybe this is a blow he deserves.

"I need a nap," he grumbles as his hands come upward to rub his face. He glances at his reflection in the mirrored wall and winces. He's met with rough stubble, a cruel reminder that he hasn't shaved in eighteen hours. There are bags under his eyes; his hair is a mess. "Great, ten years go by, and this is what I look like for the reunion?"

When the elevator slows at his floor, he goes to his room for a shower and rest. All the while, a flicker of hope ignites somewhere deep within him.

Maybe this is fate.

In her room, Willow throws her head back and laughs. It is not a nice laugh. It is throaty and desperate and roars out of her like the rumble of close thunder. Nothing about meeting Chase in an elevator is funny. Nothing about realizing she'd missed and craved him is funny, but she laughs as she tiptoes around the space of her hotel room.

"What's going on?" Lina asks as she drops to the edge of the bed. Her eyes scan the room and then rest on Willow, who's stopped laughing. Instead, she's pacing the room, her hands folded absently against her chest.

Willow doesn't answer. She continues to pace around the room, the question of her sanity coursing through her mind. She's convinced that the universe is playing a cruel trick on her. Out of all the scenarios she'd spent the past decade piecing together in her mind, this one had never occurred to her. She'd read somewhere that the world was small and karma was patient, but she'd never really thought much about it until today.

Perhaps one cannot outrun their past if they've left it unfinished, she thought.

"Hey, Willow?" Lina tries again, confused by the swift change of emotions. "What's going on with you?"

Willow says nothing, but she stops pacing. Instinctively, she laces her fingers together and bites down hard on her lower lip.

"You wanna sit down, maybe?" Lina asks and taps dutifully on the bed by her side. It would be a welcome invitation if the memory of Chase's face wasn't drowning it out.

Sighing, Lina gets up from the bed and pushes forward to take Willow's palm in hers. Gently, she squeezes until Willow blinks and registers Lina's presence.

"What's going on, Wills?"

"A ghost. I think, surely. Has to be." Willow shakes her head and swallows. "I mean, it's been ten years."

Lina furrows her brows. "The guy in the elevator?"

Willow nods and backs away to the window.

"Who was that?"

Willow hesitates. She hasn't said his name in years. Even though the memory of him sometimes comes back in blurry waves, she always avoids saying his name. But she knows she has to say it now.

"His name is Chase Kennedy." There's an awkward pause. She lifts her chin, resolute. It has to be said. "And he is my ex."

Lina drops to the edge of the bed again and crosses her legs, looking slightly nonplussed at this, her posture suggests, somewhat anticlimactic revelation. "That's it?"she half laughs and half sighs in relief. "For a moment there, you really scared me."

"Why now? What did I do to deserve this?" Willow places her hand against her chest and bends forward. "Why did he have to look so—"

Lina interrupts her, her lips half curled in an arch smile and her voice slightly coy, "Fucking *delicious?*"

Willow rolls her eyes. "Not helping, Lina."

Lina pushes herself off the bed; this time, Willow knows the reason even before Lina speaks.

"How about I give you some time alone?" Lina asks, gently grabbing Willow by the shoulders. "To settle in, gather your thoughts."

Willow nods, visibly exhausted. "Thank you, Lina."

"Don't mention it," Lina says, wrapping Willow in a brief but fierce hug of the kind that only best friends can give or are entitled to. "Give me a shout if you need anything," she mumbles into Willow's ear. Willow smiles wanly, her chin cradled on Lina's shoulder, returning the hug before seeing her out.

Once she's alone again, Willow finds herself swimming in her guilt. Snippets of the past when she'd left Chase rush to the forefront of her mind. In an instant, she feels pulled back to that fateful night.

Ten years ago...

After she'd left him in the yard, Willow had hung back and watched Chase through the bars on the back gate. She couldn't bring herself to go, but she didn't have the heart to make her presence known.

Each call of her name as he wept for her was a punishment she could not help but feel she deserved. She'd broken him, and now her feet wouldn't let her escape the scene before her...*caused by her*. Instead, she'd watched as the heart of her first love shattered, her own breaking with it.

He'd tried to call her—at that very moment in fact—but when his name lit up the screen of her phone, she'd turned it to silent. She'd let it ring repeatedly, not letting her thumb swipe across the screen to welcome his voice.

"Willow, please," he'd say in every message he'd left for her for over the following year. *"I love you."*

When the year was up, the messages had stopped, but the love she'd held for him hadn't.

Now, he's here, and Willow knows that there is no way she can hide from this—not again. He's found her. The idea of meeting him in London, *of all places*, after a decade apart builds tension within her, the kind that is almost certain to set

21

her heart on fire and burn her with its treacherous awakening, like a long dormant volcano sending out its first ominous puffs of smoke after generations of inactivity.

I could call Mom, she thinks. *If Chase has relocated here, she must know. She keeps tabs on him, I'm sure.*

The last time she spoke with her, the conversation had started with, "Guess what Jill said about Chase the other day?" and had ended with Willow saying, "You should stop being friends with my ex-boyfriend's mom; it's weird."

Willow shakes the memory away. *There is no way these could all tie down to the same thing.*

But somewhere, deep, deep inside, there is hope.

Sometimes, Willow imagines that he might still love her as he did back then. Sometimes, like now, she holds out hope that they will find their way back to each other. But sometimes, also like now, her hope is quashed by the realization that *she* is the one who broke *him*.

Willow sighs and lifts her chin. She shouldn't be afraid of meeting him again; she shouldn't even entertain the thought. But she can't help it.

Would he even be interested in seeing me again?

Raking a hand through her hair, she steadies herself. She knows she'll exhaust herself further if she continues pacing anxiously. All she wants is for the guilt to end.

Her mind muses on the possibility of going out to find him. She wants to see him again but doesn't know what to expect. She takes a deep breath and decides that the hotel is enormous and the chances they'll meet again are slim.

The air in the room suddenly feels stuffy. There are two twin dehumidifiers in the room, but she's overwhelmed with the raging stampede of memories and decides only a walk will clear her head.

She hesitates to press the button when she reaches the elevator lobby on her floor, anxious about stepping back into the box. She eyes the adjacent door leading to the stairwell and weighs her options. The likelihood of running into him again is slim, but the possibility of running into him on the stairs? Even slimmer.

She smiles, proud of her genius, and pushes herself through the door to the stairwell only to hit what she thinks at first is a wall.

Perhaps if she was paying attention to her surroundings, she would have looked through the stairwell door window and seen that it is already occupied. She looks up as the stranger turns around and, when their eyes meet, her stomach drops.

"Willow," Chase says, his voice a low, resonant boom yet still somehow laced with a tone of surprise. It appears he's had the same thought as her.

For a second, she doesn't recognize her own name. On his lips, her name sounds foreign, so new she forgets it's hers. She likes how he calls out to her though, as if they can peel away a decade of wasted time and betrayal.

There's a longing within her, a desire to lean into him as he holds her by the arms and searches her gaze. But all too soon, reality sets in, and with it, panic.

"Oh!" she squirms away from his touch and steps back until she finds herself against the door. Chase reaches for her, but she puts her hand up to stop him. "No, don't do that."

"Sorry," he says softly. It breaks her heart to hear that word from his lips. He's not the one who should be sorry.

The room feels smaller now that they are alone, and there is so much to say. Too much perhaps. Willow used to imagine how their reunion would be. Probably in a gallery, she thought. Looking up at the face of the man she once loved, Willow wonders if he still likes paintings and watching the sublime glow of sunsets. He used to call them art in its best form.

Chase, meanwhile, fills his lungs with air and wills himself to calm down as the tension between them threatens to rise. Here she is in front of him and, with her, the choice to leave or stay. His attempt to collect himself is moot as her scent invades his nose. Honeysuckle and lavender dance in his nostrils, weakening his knees.

Crossing his arms, Chase pinches himself through his sweater, bringing him back to reality. But this is a short lived victory. The moment his gaze meets hers, he loses himself again, adrift in the endless nickel, blue, and green swirls of her eyes. Fitting, considering all she'd done to him; he'd always thought they resembled a stormy sky.

Willow stares back at him, curious and calculating, unsure if she should be the one to break the ice but confident that she shouldn't run. Chase is the first to speak, and when he does, she notices the warm and comforting presence she had always seen there radiating from him.

"I guess the stairwell won't be offering the refuge we thought it would, huh?" he asks. The hint of a smile plays on his lips but doesn't fully break free.

"I think the universe might have other plans," she laughs, almost apologetically, shaking her head.

Willow's laughter startles Chase. She looks beautiful and wild, and though there is palpable hurt in the space between them, he finds himself roped in once she begins to laugh. It's the way the laughter rolls out so careless and unaffected. It's a sound that becomes a stepping stone for him to meet Willow at her level despite its seeming fragility. And even though this idea of simultaneous fragility and support should be ridiculous, it works. He joins Willow in her unrestrained laughter until they are both out of breath, stopping just short of that moment when laughter becomes painful.

Finally, he whispers, slightly out of breath and wiping tears of joy from his eyes, "Some things never change."

Willow sighs, takes a moment to catch her breath, and glances down at her feet. When she looks up at him, she thinks he is still breathtaking, maybe even more so with the benefit of time. The beautiful boy she'd loved had matured into the beautiful man she'd deserted. She shakes her head to let go of the thought and eyes him. "This is weird, right?" she asks. "I mean, of all the—how is—"

She doesn't have the words. Her cheeks flush, and she drops her gaze.

Chase steps closer to her. "Why are you so nervous?"

Even now, he can read her like no one else can. Despite the concern in his voice, she doesn't think there's any way he can possibly be serious in asking this question. She should say something but can't speak because he has a hold on her. His eyes warn her that, if she gets too close, she might just get sucked in, losing herself in them.

"Come out with me," he says.

He flusters her with his daring words, and when he raises his arms outward like an invitation, she knows immediately this is the end of her.

"What?"

Chase tries again. "Come and get a coffee with me."

She swallows, uncertain. "I'm not sure that's a good idea, Chase."

"And why not?"

Coffee with Chase is dangerous. Willow thinks of about ten thousand different excuses ranging from the painfully honest *"Because I might ask you to pretend that I didn't leave you ten years ago and beg for a redo"* to the less plausible *"I've just had a psychic premonition that my mother is in danger, and I need to check on her"*. But what she really wants to tell him is that he still bothers her with his smoldering green eyes and his full, sensual lips and his devilish grin. She wants to say she misses and wants him back, but knows how awkward it'll be if she does.

Instead, she says, "I don't drink coffee anymore." It's an excuse that falls short. Very short.

He steps fully into her personal space and Willow rediscovers the sweetness of his body being so close to hers. "That's bogus, and you know it," he argues. "You could outdrink both Gilmore girls."

He still knows her as if nothing has changed. Willow's excuse withers and dies.

"Okay, fine," she agrees, if only because she secretly wants to anyway. She nearly starts to roll her eyes but stops when she sees how his face lights up.

"After you, Sweets," he says, opening the door, gesturing for her to step through it.

Willow pauses and arches an eyebrow. It's dangerous to play the same game as him, but she likes how he switches to the nickname he used to call her back when they were still lovers. She looks up at him, and he winks.

This might just be the start of something that could burn her if she isn't careful, but perhaps, Willow thinks to herself, she can indulge in just a little warmth.

3

The Things We Won't Say Out Loud

THE BELLS AT THE ENTRANCE of the coffee shop jingle when Chase pushes the door open. He holds the door for Willow and she mutters something almost inaudible under her breath. The strong aroma of coffee beans fills his nose as they step further into the café. It hums with the faint conversations of strangers.

He hopes that he isn't making a mess of their first meeting in years but doesn't say anything to Willow as they approach the counter. A barista comes to the till and takes their order.

"I'd like an Americano and a caramel latte with oat milk for my friend here."

The barista flashes a friendly smile. "What's the name on the order?"

"Chase," he replies. Once he pays, the barista tells them to sit anywhere they'd like.

Willow leads Chase to the free booth by the window and slides down into it. He sits across from her and smiles softly to himself. Underneath the table, he imagines she's crossed her legs in the same way she used to do.

The waiting is the hardest because neither of them knows what to say to ease the tension. Willow is surprised by the familiarity of his gaze, how he still remembers her order after all these years, and how much she likes that he does. Here they are now, and she remembers these snippets like they are a part of her present, like a decade hasn't passed between them.

"What are you thinking about, Sweets?" he asks.

There it is again! Unable to stop the blush that creeps up her neck, she asks the first thing that comes to mind. "My order. How did you—"

He stops her with a raised hand. "You almost drained the town of caramel lattes senior year."

She laughs at how correct he is. He joins her, and it just feels good for a while, as though no time has passed. Then she says, "I can't believe you remember that."

Chase wants to tell her that he remembers everything about her. He wants to see the expression etched on her face when he tells her that he remembers their first meeting as well as their last, but he knows that it is too soon, that a statement like that could wreck both of them again. For now, he wants to enjoy this little victory.

"What can I say?" he laughs, his eyes shiny and insistent, "I'm amazing."

She leans forward and rolls her eyes. "I see you're still cocky too."

The moment is briefly interrupted when the barista brings their order. Chase thanks her as though he's always known her, and Willow shakes her head when the barista leaves.

"You were flirting with her."

"I'm terrible at flirting, you know that." There's a smile on his lips.

"You aren't," she says. "Maybe you were then, but not now."

"Is that so?" he asks and leans forward. "Am I having an effect on you, Sweets?"

She pushes back slightly against the table and takes her beverage with both hands, placing it to her lips. She lets it hover for a moment while she stares at him. Chase is different, and not just for the stubble on his chin; there is something else that she can't quite explain, but it settles there in the space between them, and, as much as she tries to let go of it, it stays.

Words hang in the air, growing increasingly insistent as the seconds slip past, but neither of them speak. They're both thinking the same thing: Maybe a café isn't the best place to talk about her betrayal or that he'd sent her a million messages she'd left unread.

Instead, Chase decides to try for small talk as old friends. He marks the boundary in his mind, a precaution so they do not cross the line from fresh start into old trouble. Small talk, he decides, is an easier pill to swallow.

"Of all the gin joints in all the world, we both end up in this one," he says, chuckling. The laughter is short, and she doesn't join him in it. He stops almost immediately and sips from his cup as well, looking a little abashed.

"It's uncanny," she agrees solemnly, looking down at her cup.

He narrows his eyes at her. Everything about the moment is awkward, but he knows he must forge ahead. "Some might call it fate," he suggests.

She looks up at him now and leans back against her chair. "What brings you here, anyway?"

He arches an eyebrow. "You really want to talk about that?"

"I don't know what to ask you, Chase."

Chase has already decided not to speak to her about the ten-year silence, at least until there is enough time and fewer people, but when she speaks to him in that low, chilly voice, something pops into his head. It is a question he's wanted to ask her for a long time, and once it comes to him again, it slips out of his lips without warning, ignoring the line he'd drawn for this conversation.

"Are you happy, Willow?" he asks. "With the way your life has gone, I mean?"

She wants to say *I'd be happier with you,* but what comes out of her lips is a tersely noncommittal evasion. "I'm happy with my career, yes."

The weight in her chest increases when she peers into those ocean eyes, which continue to watch her intently. Chase knows her well enough to catch her in a lie, and he does the moment she measures her happiness in work rather than life.

He doesn't push for more or try to force her into a conversation. Still, he can see the rigidness in her expression and the unhappiness in her eyes. And while he has nothing but well wishes for her, he finds himself almost relieved by how simpatico they are. He isn't the only one living an unsatisfactory personal life. Perhaps, just maybe, he can help change that.

"Good," he says, nodding.

She drapes an arm over her neck, rubbing it gently. He follows the movement, transfixed. Chase suddenly feels out of place both in body and mind in this café, but he doesn't want to leave for both their sakes.

"Are you?" she asks, lifting her chin in his direction.

"Happy?" he asks in an overly exaggerated tone. The laugh, he discovers, will not come, but he has a few things to say. A smile unfurls in place of the absent laughter. "You want the honest answer?"

"Do I want the honest answer?" she repeats. "I would hope you'd always be honest with me. I don't want you to lie to me today."

"Are you sure about that?" he asks with a hint of a grin.

She says nothing.

"I haven't been truly happy since you left," he offers after a few moments of hesitation.

"Chase…"

He swallows. Sometimes there are two potential ends to a conversation and Chase knows this. There are two scenarios for how this goes. The first one is that she stays, and he falls head over heels in love with her. The second is she leaves—just as she always does in his dreams—and he stops believing in the idea of love once again.

Shaking his head, he answers softly and truthfully, "That's the honest answer, Willow."

She is pale now, almost like she has always known his answer. "I'm—"

He raises his hand, interrupting her. "Let's not talk about that just yet."

She nods.

"How long are you in town for?"

Her answer is vague, but she hands it out as quickly as possible. "I'm not sure yet. My assistant and I are meeting with a client tomorrow. From there, we'll determine a timeline."

He leans forward and taps his fingers against the paper towel. "A client?"

She says, "I'm a couturier."

"A what now?"

She laughs before she answers, like she can brush away the strain with a burst of polite laughter. Still, it helps put her at ease. "It's just the fancy name for a fashion designer."

"No way?" he grins at the news, brightening by the smear of the past and the fusion of the present. "You did it!"

"I did," she says.

"I'm so proud of you, Willow."

She looks him dead in the eye, and he sees the woman he fell madly in love with.

"Thank you, Chase," she says, sipping from her cup, not quite daring to meet his eyes.

"What time is your meeting done tomorrow?"

Willow is quick this time around. "I'll be back by eleven."

"Have lunch with me," he says with a lopsided grin.

She crosses her arms over her chest and eyes him. "Was that a question or a command?"

For once, he doesn't back down. "What would you like it to be, Sweets?"

Oh! She lowers her eyes again and instinctively pushes a hand out to touch her face. "Chase, I…"

He drops his smirk and opts for a smile instead. Willow puts her hand down on the table.

The doorbell jingles and she glances past his shoulders at the newcomers because she knows that if she allows herself to look into his eyes, she will melt. He has the power to do that, and he knows it.

Chase rises to his feet and offers her a hand out of the booth. She hesitates for only a moment but finally slips her hand into his. When she's standing, he leans close to her ear and whispers, "If I can remember a coffee order, I most certainly remember exactly how to make you blush, Sweets."

Before she can respond, he drops her hand and goes to the door. He holds it open and watches her as she steps outside, welcoming the cool air as it hits her heated cheeks.

Their walk back to the hotel is silent and short. When they enter the elevator, Chase hesitates to hit a button. "What floor?" he asks, even though he knows where she got off earlier.

"Eight," she frames this like a question, but he knows it might just be because he is reading too much meaning into a seemingly ordinary thing.

They stand on opposite sides of the elevator, stealing glances, but both are unwilling to say anything. What is there to say?

For years, Chase has constantly been reminded of the past wherein he'd failed to keep her. Back then, he'd told himself it had been his fault, but with time, he realized he could not keep blaming himself for something she'd chosen.

Now, she is here in an elevator with him. She is breathtaking in more ways than one. The thought that after a decade he's found her again exhilarates him, and in the moment that follows, he does something he immediately knows is stupid, or would know if he was thinking about it. But he isn't.

He walks over to her, cupping her face in his hands. She releases a soft gasp, her eyes wide with wonder and confusion.

"Chase," she calls out his name in a whisper that threatens his sanity. It's not a question but rather a complete sentence. It's as if she knows on some level what's about to happen.

"Just once," he whispers. His eyes are wildly searching hers.

"Wh—what?" she can't push him away—even if she wanted to, she wouldn't—because his hands on her skin bring back a torrent of memories and want.

"I need to taste your lips once. Just once, Willow," the words come out in a breathless plea.

"Chase—"

Chase swallows her words when he dips his head low and crushes his lips against hers. Quickly, his tongue finds hers, and he holds her in place as he kisses her passionately. He has wanted—no, craved— this for such a long time that, now that it's in front of him, it seems surreal.

Because it is.

The elevator dings, acknowledging their arrival, and Chase realizes all too quickly that the kiss is in his head, a bull in a china shop knocking things over, creating chaos where there had once been order. *Perhaps I'm still a coward.* Willow still stands on the opposite side; the space between them now feels miles apart.

"This is me," she says with a small, unreadable smile.

"Uh—yeah, right," Chase blurts awkwardly. "I'll see you in the lobby tomorrow at twelve-thirty, right?" he asks. He can't help but make sure she still wants this. That's what happens when you carry the baggage that they do.

"I'll be there." With a light hand wave, Willow gives him an awkward goodbye and leaves the elevator. Once it closes, he lets out the breath he's been holding and rubs his hands across his face.

What the hell was that?

Although a small voice in the back of his head warns him that tomorrow might be tricky if he continues to spiral, he still wants to meet with her. *She may burn me again,* he thinks. *But just once, I want to feel her. Some things are worth burning for. She is worth burning for.*

4

Old Habits Die Hard

"I'M ON MY WAY," Willow tells Lina as she pushes the revolving door of the Wright Hotel and steps out onto the street. She's sent her friend ahead of her to save a booth for their client meeting. She feels giddy at the idea of returning to the same café that Chase had brought her to just the day before.

She desperately misses Chase. It's been less than twenty-four hours since crossing paths again, but to her, it feels like they never parted. Last night she fell asleep with a smile on her lips, replaying their short time together in her mind.

The thought of him in the elevator with her still makes her blush. The way he watched her so intently during the short ride, she couldn't recall the last time someone looked at her like that. She yearns to know what he was thinking—though if her imagination is anything to go by, she has a pretty solid guess.

It's more than that, though. How he stared at her, his eyes observant and layered with so many years, was haunting. It makes her think of him again and again. *He still knows me, and that's the most surreal part about all of this.*

She wonders if fate is real but forces herself to let that thought go. For now, Willow reckons a morning without thinking of him might be possible if she puts all her focus into the client meeting ahead.

Lina waves Willow to the booth she's secured the moment she steps into the café. The familiar aroma of coffee hits her hard and her stomach grumbles as she eyes the rows of pastries by the till on her way to her seat.

A treat could be lovely, she thinks. The moment she does, Chase's ruthlessly handsome face pops into her mind. She shakes her head, blushing. *What is wrong with me?*

"I ordered you a latte," Lina says as she greets Willow with a cheek-to-cheek peck.

"With—"

"Caramel and oat milk, I know," Lina replies, rolling her eyes. "They should be here any minute."

Willow slides into the booth beside her friend and rests her head on her shoulder, sighing. Lina pats her head and hums softly. "Are you ready for this?" she asks.

"Yeah, I feel good about it," Willow responds. This isn't her first rodeo; she's flown to meet clients before. But now, as jetlag rears its ugly head, she debates if she should've given herself an extra day to adjust to the time difference.

"No time to back out now," Lina says, gently pushing Willow upright and nodding to the entrance, where the bells by the door jingle as two women walk in. "I believe our client is here."

Willow slides out of the booth and rolls her shoulders back. "Show time."

"Willow?" the first woman, who has a short blonde pixie cut, approaches cautiously. She looks exhausted. Willow flashes a warm smile, nodding, and the woman visibly relaxes. "Hi, I'm Alexandra Sinclair."

"The wedding planner! It's great to meet you," Willow says just as the bride-to-be approaches the group. "And you must be Charlotte. Congratulations on your engagement!"

Charlotte is petite and a natural beauty. Her long auburn hair is styled into flawless waves and her wide green eyes pop against her pale skin and overly long lashes.

"I'm Willow Harris," she says and pushes her hands out for a handshake. "And this is my assistant, Lina Rose."

Charlotte's eyes light up, flecked with a variety of colors, which Willow finds intriguing. Although she doesn't understand how this is possible, she appreciates the bride's enthusiasm.

"I'm such a huge fan of yours, Willow!" Charlotte says. She moves her hands as she speaks, and Willow notes her engagement ring. The diamond must be at least three carats. "I've been following your career since your first week in Paris!"

Lina laughs. "Oh my, we have a real admirer in our midst."

Charlotte laughs and the others join in. For a moment, it feels relaxed. Then, when the laughter dies down, Willow makes a connection. "I'm honored, Charlotte."

The four settle into the booth, Alexandra and Charlotte sitting opposite Lina and Willow.

Work has always had a way of curing whatever stray thought Willow drowns herself in. Sitting across from this bride, she realizes how almost alike they are. It's not in the physical features but in how she sizes the table up, with one hand on her cup of coffee and the other on her lap. The exact way she lifts her chin when she speaks is as though she needs to be seen to be heard. Sometimes Willow is like that too, and she knows it, so she isn't bothered by Charlotte's manner.

"Let's talk about your wedding dress then, shall we?" Lina says. Willow nods, happy for the interruption.

"Yay!" Charlotte says, and then, because she thinks it is essential to add, "I am beyond ecstatic!"

"That's good—" Willow starts.

Charlotte continues, "I am thinking maybe silk and tulle, the whitest there is."

Alexandra leans forward with a slight, unfocused frown. "Darling, don't you think you should do a champagne color? It sure would complement the burgundy of the bridal party better."

Willow likes the banter but wants to use their limited time effectively. "Burgundy is the color of choice?"

It is Charlotte who answers. "Yes, my fiancé will be wearing a burgundy tuxedo."

"Love that!" Lina interjects and tries for a line. "With the right accessories, we could make pure white work with the deep red."

Alexandra agrees. "I can make the call to change the bouquets from champagne to white."

Charlotte's hands hover above the table, and when Willow looks at her, she can see the doubt spreading across her face. Suddenly she seems different, ethereal, like something out of space, and while Willow finds this strange, she doesn't complain.

"But I want them to be champagne," she pouts.

Willow breaks the chill. "Alexandra is right," she says patiently, but firmly. Sometimes you had to tell the client that they didn't really want what they thought they wanted. "The champagne will look almost yellow next to your dress."

The pause that follows Willow's words is, quite frankly, unnatural, but this time around, Charlotte is the first to break the spell. "Alright, fine," Charlotte says and then, with more emphasis, adds, "I guess the designer does know best."

Though she wants to contradict this, Willow doesn't push it. Alexandra seems grateful to have Willow in her corner regarding the decor, so if it keeps the peace, she'll play along. She retrieves her tablet from her bag and pulls up the sketch pad.

"Let's talk dress design," she says. It is Willow, of course, who suggests an elegant A-line for the fit of the dress because of how she's since perceived the bride-to-be. It's always part of her job to think of the perfect fit by observing her clients; this time is no exception.

Charlotte shakes her head quickly. "I was thinking more of a ball gown because I want to feel like a princess. Do you understand?"

Ultimately, a decision is reached: a pure white ball gown with a lot of tulle. It's not a bad choice either, and as Willow and Lina head out of the café to their room at the Wright Hotel, they are of the same mind.

"She is gorgeous," Lina says as they cross the space and move into the elevator. Willow agrees, nodding, slightly distracted, a somewhat distant look in her eyes.

Willow wonders if she'll also find him here. It would fit their pattern. She wants him here even though a part of her is afraid of what the outcome will be. It's why she breaks down when they get into her room.

"I don't know what to wear," she says, curling up in bed.

Lina shakes her head and chuckles. "I would beg to differ, considering you brought two suitcases."

From the rumpled sheets, Willow lets out a low groan. Then she lifts herself and sits instead. "Oh, I'm sorry. I didn't pack anything for spending a day with my ex-boyfriend."

"Great sarcasm, by the way," Lina mutters.

Willow rolls her eyes and covers her face with her palm. "What do I do, Lina?"

"Come here," there is a hint of maternal love when Lina speaks. "Sit down. Let me work my magic."

Willow obeys and sits on a chair Lina pulls out for her. She takes a few moments to do some breathing exercises, something she learned to do from the days when anxiety crept into her skin.

Today is no different, but then again, she'd also been the one to accept. Could she say no? Her mind is racing, and the fluttering of her heart is new, so alien she thinks it might not really be her in this body. Willow doesn't know if she can handle an afternoon alone with the man she still craves, but there is no time to back out of her word.

"What's the big deal anyway?" Lina asks as she dabs Willow's cheeks with setting powder. "It's been over a decade. Shouldn't everything be water under the bridge by now?"

Willow wants to tell her about how she'd left him standing and alone and how, for the year that followed, when he'd tried to call her, she'd sent him to voicemail. She wants to speak about how much she wants him, the desperation circling like a ghost in her heart, but she can't because she knows he'll never want her back. A decade has passed, but not the memory of leaving him behind or the feelings that come with it. She knows that there is no coming back from that.

"Willow?" Lina pauses. Then she sighs. "Are you worried because you think you might still like him?"

Willow swallows.

Lina tries again. "Are you nervous because there are still some unresolved feelings between you two?"

Instinctively, Willow runs a hand through her hair and bites down hard against her lower lips. When she speaks, she worries she might cry. "We never really broke up, Lina."

"What does that even mean?"

Willow swallows and shuffles her feet. "I left him. He asked me to marry him, and I left him right then."

"What?" She doesn't hide her surprise.

"He proposed, and I left him there," Willow whispers as she drops her gaze.

Lina stumbles back and clutches her chest. "Are you serious? You haven't spoken since?"

"I never returned his calls," says Willow.

"Why not?"

"I was ashamed and heartbroken."

When Lina asks why she'd reject his proposal in the first place, Willow folds in half and begins to tremble. Voicing the past like this makes her feel sick. The memory is still ingrained in her head and she feels selfish and guilty again. Still, she

49

doesn't want to forget because she knows how important it is to her sanity.

"I can't talk about it," she says. "Not now, Lina."

Lina steps forward and places her hands on Willow's shoulders. "I can respect that, of course. Tell me in your own time."

Willow nods and rests her cheek against Lina's hand. She sighs a little sadly, but she is relieved to have even a tiny part of this off her chest.

"And if I can offer you any advice for today, Willow, it is for you just to enjoy the day. Don't let this loom over you, at least for today," she drags the words out slowly for emphasis. "If he wants to talk about it, I'm sure he'll be the one to bring it up, but if he doesn't, you should at some point. You owe it to him to give him answers."

"What if—"

"Trust me, Wills; it'll be okay either way."

Willow nods. She's always trusted Lina's instincts before, so why should this time be any different? She takes a deep breath and shakes her shoulders. "Alright, I can do this."

"That's the spirit," Lina grins devilishly. "Now let's get you dressed."

In the light of the room, Willow finds herself enthralled by Lina's magic. She smooths out the satin skirt that hugs her hips like a second skin as Lina adjusts the cozy cream knit draped over her shoulders. Standing, Willow tilts her head to the side to look at her frame in the mirror.

"You look so good," Lina exclaims. "I'm pretty certain he's going to want you back... if that's what you want."

Willow's overcome with a crippling fear when she thinks back to him. The possibility of that happening is too far out. No matter how good she might look, there is no way he'll want her again. She's overcome with a crippling fear when she thinks back to him. Of course, he's asked her out to ask her about the past, and of course, she'll have no choice but to answer. He'll be done with her once he gets the answers he wants. She opens her mouth to speak but changes her mind quickly.

"I expect details," Lina says, and Willow closes her eyes to drown out the white noise.

In the lobby of the hotel, Willow makes a mistake. It is not so much a mistake as it is falling into a past habit. As she waits for Chase, her eyes catch a couple by the corner, and she has to catch her breath at their interaction, their connection. The woman is pregnant, but it's not the first thing Willow notices. It is how the man has his hands around her and how she leans into him, the two of them fitting together like pieces of a puzzle that tugs at her heart.

"I see you're still into your old habits," Chase's low voice comes from behind.

She doesn't turn immediately. She waits, instead, for the giddy rush of emotions to crash before turning. Once it does, and she turns to him, she gets caught in how he stands, only a foot away, so close it burns her.

He has a mischievous smile, one she recognizes and loves still. His hands are hidden in the pockets of his open camel coat.

"Inspiration is everywhere," she says. Her voice sounds rehearsed and out of tune. She tries again. "I didn't know you were gawking, though."

He laughs and shakes his head; she finds his expression annoyingly calm and handsome. Without trying, she realizes that Chase still has the ability to take her breath away.

"I wasn't gawking," he argues. "You're beautiful today," he says, taking her in.

She swallows and thinks about lingering over the past. She wants to go back to the time when she could love him willingly, and he could kiss her—a time when life was more straightforward. Now, there is too much pressure and guilt to ache for that with the same intensity.

Underneath his coat, Chase wears a cream cashmere sweater, and Willow absentmindedly reaches out to touch it. "So do you," she whispers. Then, shaking her head as though realizing that she's stepped out of line with the intimate gesture, she smiles a little too enthusiastically. "A cashmere sweater, hey? My how grown you are," she teases.

The briefest shadow passes over Chase's face as he remembers exactly where he got it, or more to the point, who he got it from.He feels a flash of guilty awkwardness as he briefly imagines telling Willow the sweater's origin. *Oh, this old thing? Just a Christmas gift from my fiancée. You'd love her; you guys have really similar tastes.* Chase immediately discards this for the more palatable and entirely plausible, "Mom gave it to me for Christmas last year. I'm a grown man, and she's still trying to dress me," he laughs with believable, if slightly forced, good humor, consoling himself that at least half of what he says is true.

The sound of his laughter is music to Willow's ears—which are flushed with a mixture of embarrassment and exhilaration. She finds herself wondering if it should be this easy to fall back into their old dynamic, if it should be this fun. If she deserves to have this much fun with him after everything that's happened.

53

She shakes off the thought. *Tomorrow will take care of itself. Tonight, I'm just having fun with …an old friend.* "That couple," she says, lifting her chin toward the pair she was watching earlier. There's a vacant space now. She laughs awkwardly. "As I said, inspiration is everywhere."

He steps closer and pulls his hands from his coat. "You just need to *open your eyes*," he says, lifting his fingers in air quotes, earning him an eye roll from Willow. He raises his brow, his expression suddenly serious. "I remember, Sweets."

Willow opens her mouth to say something, but nothing comes out. Chase intervenes, filling the silence by suggesting they start their outing.

A car is waiting. He opens the door and gestures for her to go in first. She starts laughing. "Your chivalry is still uncompromising."

"Only for you," he responds.

As she slips into the car, Willow thinks of brushing a hand against his, mistaking his smiles for acceptance and him wanting her as much as she wants him. It makes her blush.

When the car pulls out onto the bustling street, Chase leans back against the seat. His expensive cologne fills up the car. Willow also relaxes and tries not to think about how closely they're sitting together in the back seat of this car for fear that she'll forget how to breathe. She imagines kissing him, the desperation in her fingers grabbing him, but she shakes her head to kill off the thought.

"What are you thinking about, Willow?" he asks, interrupting her thoughts.

Ordinarily, Willow is far from being shy, but with Chase so near after so long apart, she can't help but feel this way. She glances at him and notes the seriousness in his expression. Her cheeks grow wildly pink when she looks away and begins to knit her fingers on her lap.

"Nothing," she lies. She can't tell him now that she wishes to kiss him. "It isn't important."

"Still uncomfortable around me, huh?" He turns away, and she sees, for the first time, the shadow of a scar on his chin.

She reaches out for him instinctively and brushes his skin. He turns suddenly, so close that the feeling comes again.

"Y-You have a scar," she whispers.

He pulls back first. "I had a little accident. It was so long ago I don't even remember."

She pulls her hands back. "I'm sorry."

Quietly, he asks, "What for?"

She doesn't answer, and he doesn't press her.

5

The Special in the Ordinary

THE RESTAURANT CHASE CHOSE sits on the corner of two busy streets in Covent Garden. If she'd come alone, Willow would've taken a moment to snap a photo of the unique architecture. Her brother, Adam, is an architect who's always looking for inspiration. Instead, she resists the urge and follows Chase into the building.

A hostess leads them to a table by the window and waits for them to settle across from one another before she hands them the menus. "Can I get you started with any drinks?"

Chase answers quickly, thankful for the interruption. "Water for now—sparkling," he says, then quickly adds, "We'll order our drinks when we order our meal."

"Of course," she says and moves away.

Willow rests her chin on her hand as she watches the activity on the street outside. She can feel Chase's eyes on her and suppresses a blush. Clearing her throat, she sits up and meets his stare. "How did you find this place?"

Chase leans back against the chair and presses a slight smile across his face. She would've leaned across the table and pulled him in for a quick kiss in another life. But too much time has passed; she believes a move like that would only push him away.

"I found it the first time I came to London a few years back," Chase answers. "I like the environment here; it never changes."

"Oh?" She leans forward on her elbows, "Are you in London often?"

He arches an eyebrow at her sudden interest but answers nonetheless. "Yeah, my work sends me here a lot. There's quite a few start-ups in and around London. Did you know that?"

"That doesn't—"

Willow stops when a waitress approaches the table. She sets their waters down and smiles warmly at them. "Are you ready to order?"

"Oh," Willow realizes she's forgotten to check the menu. She blushes as she picks it up and scours through. "Hmmm."

"I can give you a few more minutes," the waitress offers. She has other patrons to attend to anyway.

Willow shakes her head and looks at Chase. "You've been here a lot, right? Why don't you order something for me?"

Chase doesn't need to be asked twice. He pulls the menu from Willow's hands and looks at the waitress. "Garden burger for her and I'll take the fish and chips. And we'll take an extra basket of chips, please."

"And to drink?"

"Two pale ales, please."

"Very well," the waitress says.

After the waitress is gone, Willow folds her hands and raises a threaded eyebrow. "An extra basket of chips?"

Chase laughs and fires back, "As if you're going to be satisfied with one measly serving of fries." Willow opens her mouth to retort, but he already knows what she'll say, so he adds, "You're not stealing mine."

She covers her chest in mock horror, "How dare you insinuate I would do such a thing!"

"Oh really?" he leans forward and rests on his elbows. "You wouldn't?"

Willow doesn't respond because the truth is that she would. But she doesn't want to admit defeat, so instead, she crosses her arms and leans back in her seat, earning another laugh from Chase, which makes her expression soften. His laugh is music to her ears and worth the callout.

As a comfortable silence falls over them, neither can deny that this feels more like a romantic setting than anything else.

Their chemistry is devastatingly fragile and echoes through the space around them. Willow mirrors Chase and rests her elbows on the table again.

It's surreal to think that they're sitting here, in the same place, together. She never thought she'd get a chance like this, and now that she has, she wants to know everything about who he's become. But she's afraid to ask the big questions, so she opts for the safer subjects.

"You mentioned you come here a lot for work because of the start-up culture," she says. "What is it that you do?"

He nods knowingly and decides to play along. "I work as a lawyer specializing in intellectual property. I focus on assisting startups with their patent rights and providing guidance on copyrights, moral and publicity rights, trade secrets, and legal protection against competitors."

"That sounds like the perfect fit for you," Willow says, smiling sheepishly. "You always were drawn to the new, fresh ideas."

He wonders if she means something else but doesn't pursue that thought. "I was."

"When did you decide to pursue law instead of medicine?" she asks. "I thought you wanted to become a doctor. Follow in the family business, that sort of thing."

"That was the plan, initially," he agrees. "But I became friends with some people who were in law school, and they opened my eyes to a whole different side of science."

Knee-deep in conversation with Chase, Willow begins to find it increasingly hard to pull away from him. "How did your parents take that?"

"They were pretty pissed." There's laughter in his voice. "Mom especially, but it's not her life; it's mine. And I love my career."

A sense of pride and excitement fills Willow's chest as she listens to him and she doesn't hide it—even if the grin she's wearing is a little cheesy. "Wow, I'm really happy for you, Chase."

Maybe she no longer reserves the right to tell him that; maybe her approval doesn't mean anything to him anymore, but she refuses to keep it to herself.

Heat creeps up Chase's neck at the compliment. "That means a lot to me, Willow," he says softly before crossing his legs. "Tell me about your career. You're one of the top designers, right?"

She feigns surprise. "How did you know that?"

"Oh, I'm just assuming."

"You Googled me, didn't you?" Willow rolls her eyes and adjusts her leg space. Her foot brushes against Chase's leg, but neither tries to pull away.

"I'm not at liberty to say," he shrugs. "I can neither confirm nor deny," he says with mock seriousness.

When Willow begins to laugh, Chase holds his breath. It's not the first time he's hearing the sound of her hearty laughter or the first time he's holding his breath out of nervousness with her so close to him, but it's the first time he thinks about running away.

He's well aware of how this story ends, of how she leaves again, and how he ends up pining for a love that should have ended long ago. He wants to run and hide away from the world, and this craziness makes him forget, momentarily, that she is still here with him.

"Chase?" She taps his arm, and he flinches suddenly. "Are you okay?"

"I'm fine," he says with a quick smile. "Please continue."

She looks skeptical but doesn't push him. "I wouldn't say I'm one of the *top* designers. But my career did catapult fairly quickly into the fast lane."

"And now you travel the world to meet with clients?" he asks, leaning back against the chair and crossing his arm against his chest.

"Something like that, yeah," she says. "I love the freedom this career gives me. I get to travel all over for Fashion Week in different cities. But I also have freedom in the sense that I get to create art each and every day. It's more than designing clothes for me. It's expressing myself in any way I want."

Chase tries to imagine her as someone ready to stand still but cannot. The more he thinks of the past, the more hurt and inexplicably alone he feels even with her around. Still, he tries his best to forget and be in this moment with her. "That's amazing, Willow. You've done really well for yourself."

She nods, happy. "That means a lot coming from you."

The waitress brings two pale ales and sets them on the table. When she leaves, and they're alone again, Chase asks, "So, with all the jet setting, where's home for you these days?"

"I was living in New York up until six months ago," Willow says, raising the glass. She takes a slow sip before continuing, "I needed a change of place, but I didn't want to give up the city life, so I found a cozy little house in Chicago and opened a store location downtown."

Chase lifts his drink but doesn't take a sip from it. Instead, he uses it to hide his frown.

"What a coincidence," he mutters. The realization that finding her after so long won't guarantee him the closure he's been looking for sets in. He'll be lucky to get anything remotely close to that now.

A small smile tugs at the corners of her mouth. "You moved to Chicago?"

"I moved there after getting accepted into DePaul University," he answers brusquely, "when I decided to study law."

"How did your parents feel about you leaving Portland?" Willow asks. It must have been quite a shock for Jillian Kennedy to learn that her son not only didn't want to become a doctor but planned to move out of the state as well.

"Oh, they were angry. But, like I said," he shrugs, "it's my life."

Willow takes another sip and then sets her glass back down. She glances outside at the honking cars and strangers walking by and thinks back to that night behind the big house, the garden lights strung up so artistically, so vividly real. "What are the chances we ended up in the same city after all this time?"

Chase sighs. "If that's not fate, I don't know what is."

Their waitress, interrupting the conversation with timing that is either impeccable or terrible depending on how one chooses to look at it, approaches their table. "Here are your meals," she says as she sets the food down. "Let me know if you'd like anything else."

The moment they're left alone again, Willow reaches across the table and plucks a fry from Chase's plate. He gasps in mock surprise.

"This is why I ordered the extra basket," he says, shaking his head and biting back a smile.

She shrugs, smirking.

The food is delicious and they fall into a comfortable silence. Willow's caught off guard by how normal being here with him feels. It's ordinary yet special as if this is how they've always been.

Sometimes, she thinks she could have taken him with her. Maybe they wouldn't be here as two strangers reconnecting if she had. Perhaps they'd be here as lovers on vacation.

Deep down, she knows the love that should've ended years ago is still present; strong, heavy, and desperate.

"What are you thinking about?" Chase asks in an attempt to reel her back to him. She simply shakes her head, unwilling to confess, so he tries a different route. "What do you say we get out of here and take a walk?"

6

Confessions at Sunset

CHASE FLEXES HIS FINGERS, fighting the overwhelming desire to reach for Willow's hand as they walk side by side. Eventually, he opts to shove his hand into his pocket.

Stealing a glance, he catches her eye for only a moment because she blushes and quickly looks away. He begins to wonder about the attraction between them and if, like him, she longs to make their time together last longer.

Does she regret coming out with me? he asks himself. *If not now, later?*

Chase wants her to be closer to him, to take her in his arms and kiss every inch of her beautiful face, but he knows he can't because she's not his. Hell, her heart could even belong to someone else.

Seeing her again after so long hasn't given him a chance to think of this, but somehow, being here with her has made him aware of many different possibilities. What if there is someone else in the picture? The probability of this is high; as such, Chase becomes increasingly agitated about it even though he knows he has no right to.

After all, he has a fiancée. *Dammit. Damn the luck.*

Regardless of how he and Char feel—or don't feel—about each other, he's still spoken for. And yet, being here with Willow only makes him wish he wasn't. The endless 'what-ifs' play through his mind as they walk side by side. What if he wasn't betrothed? What if he'd reunited with Willow sooner? What if he was engaged to her instead?

What if? What if? What if?

"Chase?" Willow calls again, pulling him out of his thoughts this time. "You seem kind of distracted today."

"I'm sorry, what was that?" He tries for a smile, holding his anxiety in.

She giggles. "I was going to suggest walking across that bridge," she points to one of the Golden Jubilee Bridges, mesmerized by the unique design of the tall steel rods that angle together to create a sort of canopy. Chase's smile grows, almost as though he's been waiting for this.

"Oh sure, definitely!"

As they climb the steps to the bridge, avoiding fellow pedestrians who are ignoring the arrows that instruct the direction they should be walking, Willow gasps as she takes in the view. The River Thames is busy with different boats coming to and from either side of the bridge. Ahead of them, the cityscape is breathtaking and quickly, she pulls out her phone to capture the scenery. "This view is beautiful, Chase!" Her voice is full of wonder.

Walking beside the woman of his dreams, Chase is powerless, walking beside her as if compelled. He isn't sure he could stop walking with her even if he wanted to, which, of course, he doesn't. He smiles as he observes her, allowing the curiosity to consume him.

Instinctively, his hands squeeze the flesh of his opposite arm, a pinch, to assure that he is indeed here with her. And as the wind brushes the nape of Willow's neck, her scent fills his nose, and he wonders if this is the beginning of a dream or a glimpse of heaven.

Either way, he wants to stay here like this forever.

"Tell me something about yourself, Willow," he says suddenly. Maybe he should stop himself from learning about who she's grown into, but he longs to know everything.

She arches an eyebrow, but there is laughter in her eyes. "What would you like to know?"

"Anything," he says. *Everything,* he thinks. "What's your favorite part of your career?"

She does not hesitate. "Besides the freedom to create?"

He nods. "Obviously."

"Honestly, I love a lot of things about my career," she says. "Aside from the freedom to create whatever I want; I also get to travel a lot. I've met a lot of interesting people along the way, too. Take today's client, for example. The way she talked about her fiancé and the love in her eyes when describing their story was phenomenal. It's an honor to be in a position to hear these stories from clients."

"So you're finding inspiration in everyone you meet?"

On the surface, the question sounds natural, innocuous enough, but beneath it all, Willow can tell that he means her life in the great scheme of things, the architecture of the universe. With his seemingly innocent question, he's really asking her if she's happy watching people.

She wants to tell him the truth about how sometimes she wants more, but instead, her voice circles over a vague answer. "Exactly, Chase, or at least I'd like to think so."

After all their history together, he can see, underneath her answers, something devastatingly sad.

She continues, "What about you? You've told me what you enjoy about your career, but what about when you're not working? What do you do in your spare time?"

In truth, there's a myriad of options available to Chase, and in all of these, there's an open option to merely scratch the surface. But when he looks at her again and he catches a glimpse of the girl he's always known, he falls into step and speaks from the raw, aching mess that is his heart.

"Actually, I write," he says.

She seems taken aback by this and pauses; one hand raised outward as though she might be waiting for something more. "You write?"

"I know, I know," he laughs childishly. "Unexpected, right?"

She lifts her eyebrow before she speaks. "Well yeah, you hated English in high school."

He runs a hand through his hair and swallows. Up ahead, a pigeon flies past and lands softly on the railing, its spindly legs holding on tightly. Willow points to it, giggling. When she turns back to him, the conversation continues like it never ended in the first place, picking up right where it left off.

"I needed one more credit in my first year of university, so I chose a random English course. I figured it would be an easy pass, just reading literature. Well, it turns out I had signed up for a creative writing course. It was wild, but I actually really enjoyed it. And I did well, too. It turns out heartbreak can really help your creativity."

Shit.

71

Chase pauses and licks his lower lip. Her eyes do not speak to him, but he feels almost swatted by his own words. Perhaps he shouldn't have said it like that.

"I'm sorry, Willow. I didn't mean to make you uncomfortable."

She shakes her head and glances down at her open palm. "It's alright. I know I have some explaining to do."

"Let's not talk about that right now," he says, cutting her short with a dismissive flick of his wrist. But it's not condescending, just conciliatory; she knows what he means.

She nods.

He smiles and links arms with her. She gasps softly but does not pull back, and for a while, Chase recognizes the appeal of this; he finds it beautiful to be here with her and not have to fear the future. But then he pulls his hands away and pushes them into his coat pockets again.

"Tell me how you like London," he steers the conversation forward.

"Well, I've only been here for two days," she replies thoughtlessly.

Chase waits, his etched eyebrows doing the talking. She laughs and knits her fingers in front of her.

"But so far, I'm really enjoying it," she says.

Willow's eyes widen when they step off the bridge and onto The Queen's Walk path. "Is that—"

"The London Eye, yes," Chase replies. The Ferris-wheel-type structure is unbelievably massive. The way it towers over everything else within its vicinity never fails to surprise him, no matter how many times he sees it.

She gasps, clasping her wrists like a little child, and as he watches her skip a few paces ahead of him, he can't help but think about the danger in such beauty. He doesn't want the wonder in her gaze to stop, so he jogs toward her and smirks.

"What do you say we take a spin?"

"What, up there? Really?"

"Why not?" he shrugs and checks his watch. The sun is beginning its slow descent, illuminating the dusky sky with vivid color. It'll be dark soon, he realizes, but the queue for the Eye isn't long. They have time. He offers her his hand, and she's all too eager to accept it. "Come on, let me show you one of the best views in London."

"Wow, Chase..." Willow's voice trails off as she stares at the sky awash with pinks and oranges.

Standing there with her, in one of the London Eye's pods, his eyes search her skin, her hands, the nape of her neck. Every immaculate inch of her. "I told you that this is the best view," he says only half sure that he's talking about the horizon.

"It really is," she says as she turns away from the window to face him. "I don't think I'll ever see a prettier view." Then, adding a smirk, she says, "Thanks for ruining all my future sunsets."

Chase chuckles and runs a hand through his hair. He wants to tell her he hopes she spends the rest of her life watching the sunset and thinking of him, but he knows not to push his luck. So instead, he attempts to change the subject.

"How are your parents these days? And your brother and sister?" He figures moving the conversation to her family will bring them back to safer ground.

"Brynn, Adam, and my dad live in New York," she says. "Mom hasn't left Portland since the divorce, though."

Chase's face drops. Willow's response is so calm, so nonchalant, but he feels foolish for asking in the first place. "Shit, I've put my foot in my mouth again, haven't I?"

"It's alright, Chase," she laughs, and for the first time, he can't tell if she means it. "You, of all people, shouldn't be surprised."

"I guess you have a point," he agrees. "What made them finally call it quits?"

She shrugs and looks like she's about to make a joke but changes her mind. "Honestly, I think it was Brynn and me moving out. They were only together for our sake. Adam was still there, but I think it was easier to end things with only one kid at home. The nest was more or less empty, and they realized there was nothing left between them."

"They separated after you moved out for college?"

"Yeah."

"Willow..." he swallows, unsure. "That was shortly after you left me. Why didn't you tell me?"

She pauses, awkward, and faintly he can see tears shimmering in her eyes. He does not want to push her further away but wants to know what she means.

"We weren't exactly talking at that point," she whispers.

Chase takes a deep breath as the memory of her haunting betrayal slithers upward from his stomach like a snake, a python or a boa constrictor maybe, curling itself around his heart and squeezing. It becomes even harder to breathe when she looks up at him. He feels the serpentine coils constrict more tightly. So he shuts his eyes and keeps his hands pressed firmly against his sides. He crosses the pod to put distance between them, but her voice stops him.

"Chase," she calls out, and it's an ambush to his sanity. *Anything but my name on her lips, please, God.*

"Two years, Willow," he says. "We were together for two years."

She takes a step toward him. "I just thought it wouldn't have been fair of me to run to you after what happened. I assumed you wouldn't want to hear from me."

"Of course, I would have wanted to see you. I called you every single day." He runs his hands through his hair in frustration and groans. "Just because you left me without saying anything doesn't mean I stopped loving you."

This is a battle between his head and his heart, but in the face of a confession as raw and honest as this, he knows of nothing else but the woman in front of him.

Chase is well aware that he should have stopped his verbal confession before it got out of hand, but for years after she left, there had been no chance of saying it aloud.

He grinds his teeth as he slips his hands around her waist and edges her in. "I've never stopped loving you."

A small smile plays on her lips, and when his hands around her become firmer, Willow rises on tiptoe and places a hand at the nape of his neck. She pulls him closer to her.

Her heart begins to pump wildly in her chest at the knowledge of his love and the idea that her feelings might be reciprocated somehow. Her eyes move from his and then lower to his lips. So, close she becomes one with him.

A whisper escapes his trembling lips as his eyes study hers.

"Willow, I—" He swallows the lump in his throat.

"Kiss me, Chase," she whispers.

He swallows again. Chase knows this is wrong, but her lips and the pleasure of being close to her run through his mind for now. He inclines his head and presses his lips to hers.

At first, the kiss is gentle, playful. But he loses control when she leans in and presses her body against his. His hands come around her neck and grab a handful of hair, tugging it passionately, but not roughly, extracting a sigh of contentment from Willow's lips.

The kiss is heated and far different from years ago. When he kisses her now, it isn't with the fury of leftover emotions. Oh no. Rather it is with the want of insatiable need—this kiss—and it begins to collide with his underlying fears.

It's beautiful and passionate, but it's a mistake.

He pulls away from the kiss but leans his forehead against hers. Breathlessly, he says, "Wait."

She swallows. "What's wrong?"

"I can't do this," he says simply.

He can see the tremor on her lips when she calls his name again. "Chase?"

He pulls back suddenly, releasing her waist as if she's burned him, and she thinks he's gone even though he's still in front of her.

"I'm sorry."

"For kissing me?" Her voice is low, but it carries the pain of an unspoken wound that he can't help hearing.

But still, Chase knows that he needs to be honest and true, both to himself and to her. "I shouldn't have done that."

She steps closer until her fingers tighten methodically around his hands. "What if I wanted you to?"

"Willow…" he swallows. He wants her. He needs her and yet knows there must be truth as well as need. "I can't kiss you. No matter how much I want to—how much my very soul wants me to. But I can't. I can't do that to you."

She balls her hands into fists, and he takes another step back.

"Why not?" she asks, and it feels like she is asking him a million questions all at once; questions he can't find the right answers to no matter how hard he tries because there are so many things running around in his head at the moment. His mind is a riot of activity, all his thoughts shouting so hard to be heard that he can't hear any one of them clearly.

Her eyes—usually so sparkling and mischievous, but now stormy and overcast—search his, and then, because there is nothing much else for her to do, Willow begins to tug at the sleeve of her sweater. Looking up at him helplessly, she silently urges him to explain himself, to articulate answers to the questions her lips refuse to ask.

And he does. He hates himself, hates everything about this, but he does.

"Because I'm engaged, Willow."

7

Longing for Closure

Four years ago...

CHASE WAS WELL AWARE OF his shortcomings in dealing with strangers, but in a bar with his friends, Isobel and Beck, he felt almost confident.

In fact, he felt so close to confidence that he found himself unphased by the woman at the corner table with ringlets of startlingly luminescent auburn hair who continued to watch him inquisitively. She hadn't looked away even when he'd first caught her curious gaze. And while it made him giddy with excitement, his voice and manner were even and unstrained.

The lighting in the pub was dark, but nonetheless, it somehow managed to courteously illuminate significant details about his auburn-haired admirer. She was petite and confident looking, like someone he used to know. This sense of familiarity drew him in.

Beside him, his friend, Isobel, slammed her hand against the table. Beck's pint of beer shook and spilled across the bar top, and he cursed under his breath. The auburn-haired stranger broke eye contact and watched as the yellow liquid pooled on the bar top before descending unceremoniously to the ground. Chase reached forward with a napkin and dabbed at the mess.

"Sorry," Isobel muttered. "It's just frustrating, you know? I swear if one more partner assigns me paralegal work, I'm gonna scream."

Chase noted her annoyance, and hoped he wasn't out of line when he said, "Isn't paralegal work part of your job?"

She rolled her eyes, and Chase immediately thought he must've made a mistake. "I'm a junior associate, Chase. They're treating me as a paralegal because it's one big boys' club at Goldman, Blum, and Jacobs."

Beck reached something to say and slipped a comforting hand over hers. "You'll make name partner someday, Isobel."

"Easy for you to say, old man," she bit back at him, though more out of humor than anger.

Letting the two of them hash out this debate on the mores of the business world, Chase looked up at the woman across the room again. She was no longer staring at him; instead, she was focused on her drink, but Chase found himself thinking there might just be something in the cards for him if he'd just go talk to her.

It suddenly dawned on him how long it'd been since a woman intrigued him in the way this one did, prompting him to get up, dust his hands on his trousers, and take a chance.

"I'm gonna grab another drink," he said, interrupting Isobel and Beck's ongoing debate.

"You literally have a full glass right in front of you," Beck said, doing little to hide his smirk.

But the remark fell on empty space. Chase has already left the table.

Isobel laughed, tapping Beck. "He's found someone."

"Of course he has."

At the table of the as yet nameless siren with the auburn tresses, Chase asked, "Is this seat taken?"

She tilted her head down, glanced at him through thick lashes and smiled coyly. "My my, don't you work fast?"

The first thing he noticed when she spoke was her accent, which only added to the mystery.

She is beautiful, he thought. He said, "I'm just a guy who knows what he wants."

This was a lie. Chase hadn't known what he wanted for three years. But she didn't need to know what a lost soul he was.

She leaned forward. Her smile was natural. "And what is it that you want?"

"Oh, plenty," he responds. "Your name, where you're from with an accent like that…"

He sat in the chair across from her and placed his hands on the table. His eyes took in every detail: her hands, her body, the tattoo of a rose on her waist peeking out from underneath her cropped shirt. She followed his gaze and giggled when he looked at her.

He swallowed. "The story behind that tattoo…"

"What's your name?" she asked.

He answered immediately. "Chase Kennedy."

"Charlotte Wright," she responded and sat upright. "Buy me a drink, and maybe I'll tell you the story behind my tattoo, Chase Kennedy."

"D-did you just say you're engaged?"

Willow's chin quivers, and she bites her bottom lip. She doesn't want to cry. After all, she's the one who left him—in the past, true, but it still stings, regardless.

She loves him, and only now, when she sees him and hears his confession, does she realize this. When they met again after a decade apart, she hadn't contemplated him being attached to anyone, let alone engaged. It had been selfish of her, but what could she do?

"Let me explain, please," he pleads.

She swallows and folds her hands against her chest. It becomes difficult for her to breathe and much more challenging to look Chase in the eye. Blood pounds in her ears and the anxiety tearing through the barriers of her heart threatens her sanity.

It's at this moment that she wishes for silence. Her brain is in overdrive; thought after thought, doubt after doubt, question after question, comes rolling in. This sort of thinking has always been the problem. But now? It feels a million times worse.

Looking at Chase, watching his expression change from loving and caring in one moment to guilt and shame in the next, makes her feel like someone has reached into her chest and begun squeezing her heart. The pain is beyond compare, and she has to look away.

No matter what she tries to make of this moment, Willow knows that she's lost him. Accepting it now is better than clinging to a future that'll never be hers.

A part of her wants to leave this godforsaken pod and never look back. But a more significant part of her wants to wait it out; wait until Chase's explanation to settle calmly over her like a fine mist until both can walk away without any hard feelings.

Willow doesn't want to look him in the eye because she knows she might see the fear and need that was present in the elevator and the back of the taxi, and then she will not be able to leave again. His eyes have always been her undoing; constantly watching him will break her.

Chase is the one who breaks the silence, and when he speaks, she thinks he might not be the man she has always known.

"Willow, I was a mess after you left me," he says as he rubs his jaw. "I hate admitting that to you."

She says nothing.

Chase continues regardless. "I wanted nothing more than to hate you for leaving me, but I couldn't. Even after the way you left me, I still longed for you. I—I spent a *year* trying to reach you."

This time around, he stops. The memories catch up to him, and he remembers how he'd been, waiting, his hands pressed against his phone, for a call or a text from Willow. And every day, he found himself falling further and further into the abyss of self-doubt and loneliness.

She finally looks up at him, and he sees the tears. He wants to reach across and hold her, but he knows that this is a conversation he needs to have without his hands on her body. If he holds her in his arms again or kisses her, Chase is almost certain he won't let go again.

"You spent two years etching yourself onto my heart, Willow, imprinting yourself on my soul. Then you walked away as if I was nothing."

She shakes her head and raises a hand to touch him. Instinctively, Chase pulls away. Remembering the past with her in front of him makes him so angry that she made him fall madly in love with her, only for her to leave him behind.

He doesn't hate her—not really. But being in her presence now, the grief he's been longing to express must come out.

"Chase, I—"

"You ruined me, Willow!" he interjects. His eyes are narrow and his voice is raised in a way she's never witnessed before. In the wake of her departure, he found himself adrift in a torrent of agony that had made him wish he was dead. "I became a shell of a man after you left me."

"I'm sorry," she whispers, so low it becomes indistinguishable from white noise.

"A switch flipped after I realized you would never return my calls." Chase is both angry and sad, consumed by the need to express himself to her. "I couldn't hate you, so I decided to forget you. At least I tried to forget you. But in my attempt, I lost myself."

"Oh, Chase…"

"I thought if I lost myself in someone else, I would forget about the ache in my heart that I felt every time your face came into my mind. But I was naïve, wasn't I?"

He begins to laugh, but there's a strain in his laughter, a bitterness that she instantly recognizes.

"I saw you everywhere I looked, Willow," he continues, his tone laced with resentment. "I'd hear your laugh in every room and feel your gaze in every stranger. You ruined me for anyone else. Eventually, I had to accept that although you left, you still lingered."

He pauses just as a lone tear escapes and rolls down her cheeks. "You *still* linger," he confesses softly. "After I accepted that, I felt a weight lift off my shoulders."

"And her?" Willow finds her voice now. She knows she doesn't have the right to feel this way, especially with him, but hearing him say all of this breaks her heart.

"I wasn't looking for love," he responds flatly. "Hell, I wasn't looking for anything even when I met my fiancée. At the time, neither of us wanted anything serious. But that's the way life works, isn't it? You never plan to fall for someone, but you can't stop it when you do."

Willow cleans off the tears and nods, swallowing the lump in her throat. "How long have you been engaged?"

Without hesitation, like a round from the chamber of a gun, Chase fires. "One year."

Willow falls silent again. It isn't a grand confession or anything of that sort, but it still takes her breath away. His eyes are empty pools, and, as they stare right back at her, she thinks there isn't any feeling left. It is this knowledge seeping into her that makes her breath hitch and her stomach ache.

Together, they had so many plans and dreams that anything less feels like a lie. In a way, she feels betrayed, but most of all, she feels the intense shame that stems from lost love. Her heart is breaking again, and she wonders if he's doing it intentionally, a long-delayed vengeance for the pain she's caused him.

She realizes she might be right when she sees the emptiness in his eyes at her tears. How could she not feel that way when he'd spent the day leading her on, holding her close—kissing her?

How could she not feel this way when he'd done all that only to rip her heart out the way she'd done to him all those years ago?

"Why did you kiss me?" she asks. Her voice is throaty and dull, but she asks anyway. She wants to know his reasons. "Was today a ploy? An attempt to make me feel what you felt when I left?"

He licks his lips and leans forward. "I would *never* put you through that kind of heartache, Willow."

She rakes a hand through her hair, unable to stop herself. "Then why, Chase? Why did you take me out today? Why did you kiss me?"

"Because I can't get you out of my head, Willow!" His response is loud and full of frustration. He pulls out the words like a string of lines he's rehearsed, but there's a rawness to it, which tells her he speaks out of emotion.

"Hell, when I saw you in the lobby yesterday, everything I'd been keeping under lock and key came pushing through. All the what-ifs started pouring in, and I couldn't stop them," Chase continues, shaking his head. Then, like a surrender, he adds the truth, "I wasn't trying to lead you on, Willow; I was trying to get closure."

Closure.

A word that frightens both of them because up until this moment, it's always been a fantasy, a thrust into the probability of heartbreaks but with her here and with time pausing to relive this moment with him, he realizes that he isn't ready for it.

Of course, she's devastated, but most of all, Willow knows there is no coming back from this. Defeated, she sighs deeply and extends an arm, as one offering a prize to the winner of a contest. "Well, I guess you have your closure now."

He shakes his head, and she begins to imagine if, like her, there's more he wants to explore. "I have confusion, Willow, not closure."

Frowning, she says, "What do you mean?"

Chase hesitates for a moment; he holds on to the pain and exhaustion as a stepping stone.

"I thought spending the day with you, and hearing about your life, would help me close the 'Willow' chapter in my life."

"And?" she edges him on, feeling sheepish.

"All it did was make me long for you, all of you," he responds softly.

It catches her off guard. She worries that this might become burdensome for both of them, but she likes how the warmth of his need, like hers, is still present even after all these years.

But when she looks into his eyes, Willow tries to convince herself that the startling fear she sees is only a figment of her imagination, but she knows it's more than that.

His confession of wanting her comes with a shocking reality that surpasses love and free will. It is as though his unending love is also his darkest thought.

But where does this leave us?

8

Reluctant Farewells

THE RIDE BACK TO THE hotel is slow and quiet. Chase keeps his hands away from Willow this time, and she doesn't complain.

Willow has always made up scenarios for how and when they'd meet again, but nothing is quite like this. She knows this is the end for both of them, but she doesn't want to be the person to say it aloud.

Chase has spent years and years thinking of the proper goodbye, an end to a love that was both sad and impossible, but now that the time has come, he wants more. Couldn't she see that too?

Once they reach Willow's hotel room door, Chase sighs. "This is it, isn't it?"

She looks down at her feet when she talks because she doesn't want him to see the hurt in her eyes. "You know it has to be, Chase."

"We deserved so much more than this," he says quietly.

"We did," Willow admits tearfully. "We do. But if I've learned anything, Chase, love doesn't always follow a plan. It's messy and—"

"Love?" Chase asks, a blush creeping up his neck. "Willow, do you still love me?"

When faced with the matter of love, Willow becomes nostalgic for a time that, she now realizes, has only existed in the back of her mind: the possibility of a life with him without the guilt, strain, and recklessness—a life filled with everything good, pure, and beautiful.

Looking at him now, Willow knows that she loves him far more than she's willing to admit, but she does not know if this is important enough to voice aloud, if telling him will lead to anything good.

Chase takes a step in her direction, and she sees, for the first time, a kind of seriousness that takes her by storm. He's greedy for an answer, and she realizes he won't stop *until* she answers.

"I have never stopped loving you, Chase," she replies truthfully. Maybe she shouldn't, but she feels that she owes it to him to be sincere at this moment. "But it doesn't matter anyway."

He crosses the space between them and takes her in his arms. It feels almost dangerous to touch him, to find herself so ardently wanted in this way, regardless of the consequences. His arm on her bare skin makes her giddy. If he kisses her, Willow will surely risk it all for him.

Kiss me, Chase. Choose me. Willow pleads silently—which she knows she shouldn't. *Let's run away together.*

Chase puts his forehead against hers and licks his lips. "Of course, it matters, Willow."

He links his fingers with hers, which brings back blissful memories of running through fields of flowers, of pleasant days, and passion nights, always with their fingers intertwined, and knowing above everything else that they were in love.

But this time, it's different because she knows he has someone else.

Willow swallows. Her stare, flat and metallic, takes in Chase's hands, and as his words play in her head, she realizes something important: Chase is gone. His heart is no longer available; there is no space for her.

He kisses the top of her head again, but she pulls her hand from his and places it on his chest to push him away.

"Please don't make this harder than it already is, Chase," she whispers.

He lets out a defeated sigh and takes a step back. He wants to tell Willow they can try to work it out but thinks of Charlotte instead. It takes him by surprise to think of someone else while he is with the woman he loves, but he knows the truth, and it is not as complicated as he wants to believe: his heart is claimed by another, and although things have been frigid lately, he owes it to Charlotte to try.

"Willow, I—"

"Well, well, well. Look what the cat dragged in!" Lina's teasing voice cuts through their moment, and she stops short when she sees Chase step away from Willow. She quirks a threaded brow. "Am I interrupting a goodnight kiss? Don't let me stop you, kiddos."

Lina covers her eyes and turns around, whistling to herself, obviously enjoying the situation.

Willow wants to tell her not to bother, but she remains silent when she meets Chase's heated gaze. *Kiss me, Chase. Choose me.*

"I should..." Chase begins.

Let's run away together, Willow wants to say it, but instead, she rubs the back of her neck and responds with a soft "Yeah..."

"Goodnight, Willow," he says, turning away from her.

"Goodbye, Chase."

For a moment, there is hesitation in Chase, but he quickly shakes it off.

Willow watches him walk away, thinking that he might turn around, but when he doesn't, she's unsure if it's the aftermath of his confession or his not turning around that breaks her heart.

Once he's gone, Lina wraps an arm around her shoulders. "Come on, Wills."

In her room, Willow climbs into bed and covers her face with her palm.

"What happened?" Lina asks, standing above her.

Willow doesn't answer for the longest time, but her voice is cracked and out of tune when she does. "He's engaged!"

Willow sits upright, and Lina pulls her into an embrace.

"Oh, Willow, I'm so sorry," she whispers.

Willow is shivering but not from the cold. "I love him, Lina," her voice curls around the words like they are strange and unfamiliar. "I've never stopped. I ruined him, and he found someone better."

The idea of meeting him again has crossed her mind several times, but never had she imagined so complicated a meeting. Never had she imagined that it would hurt her in this way. But when she thinks back to his status and his painfully honest confession, she suddenly feels very tired.

Lina knows her all too well, but when Willow breaks down, crying and shivering, she misses a step, taken aback by the sheer force of her friend's emotional outpouring. Still, she'll say anything to help with the pain she knows Willow is feeling. "I know it doesn't seem like it right now, but I promise it will get easier."

"I...don't...think...so," Willow manages to gasp in between sobs.

"Go take a hot bath, put on your pajamas, and I'll return with reinforcements."

Willow shakes her head almost immediately. "I really just want to be alone right now, Lina."

"That's fine, honey." Anything for her, she reasons. "I'll go pick up the necessities for stage one of heartache and leave you for the night. I'll be back in a bit."

When she finds herself alone, Willow feels a strange sense of detachment accompanying the realization that her time with Chase has finally and irrevocably come to an end.

It takes Chase every ounce of strength not to look back at Willow as he walks away. All his willpower and courage melted at the sight of her in the hotel lobby that first day, but, seeing her at the door, Chase is tempted to stay.

Now, alone in his room, he thinks about returning to her. He knows it might become problematic, but being away from Willow again, he begins to understand why it is so hard to let her go. He's shaken from this thought when his phone rings. He contemplates disregarding it for a while but then sees that it's Charlotte calling.

Her voice is weirdly high-pitched and enthusiastic when he picks up, something he does not often notice in her. "Darling?"

"Hey, honey. Sorry I didn't call you; I just got in."

"From where?" her question nearly sounds accusatory, but then again, he can't exactly tell her about the woman who'd broken his heart ten years ago.

He settles for a lie instead, and although he hates the casual deception, he also knows—or at least believes—that it is necessary. "I had another meeting. Arina called me right after I finished up with Williams."

She takes a while to answer. In the silence, Chase imagines her thinking, her thoughts going back and forth between believing and disregarding what he's told her. And he can't blame her for this.

She finally says, "Oh, alright."

And he lets out the relieved breath he did realize he'd been holding.

She continues regardless. "Well, as luck would have it, dinner does work for me tonight. I'm just grabbing a cab now. I should be at the hotel in twenty minutes."

Chase pauses for a moment, allowing himself to make a decision and find his voice, pitching it to a carefully neutral tone. "Actually, honey, I was wondering if we could talk privately. Maybe we could just have dinner here?"

"Sure, Darling, we can order room service, like old times," she replies immediately. "Meet me in the lobby?"

"Alright then," he says. "I'll see you in twenty, Char."

One of the things Chase always admired about Charlotte is how strict she was with her time. It's something he learned about her on their second date. Never, in all the years they've been together, has she been late.

He, on the other hand, he'd once been five minutes late picking her up. Chase had taken her down to a beach, and, as they stared into the deep blue sea, she told him that if they were to continue, she needed him to value the importance of being on time.

Then, she'd told him she hoped he would because she liked him. It was different from before—this being liked—and it took him by surprise. He liked her too, but perhaps there had been a reason for them to like each other back then.

"You look lovely, Char," he tells her twenty minutes later. On. The. Dot. And she does look lovely. Meticulously put together, as always, wearing an oversized white wool coat. Her hair is styled in soft waves that remind Chase of Old Hollywood.

She smiles sincerely and says, "Thank you, Darling."

He steps right to her and offers his arm, "Shall we?"

Charlotte's melodic laugh echoes through the nearly-empty lobby as Chase leads her toward the elevators. He's so engrossed in her that he doesn't notice Willow's friend watching them from the concierge desk, staring daggers at them with such force that, were Chase aware of her gaze, he would be grateful that the expression 'If looks could kill' has no literal effect in the real world.

In his room, Chase goes to the writing desk and picks up the room service menu. He reckons that they can take advantage of the privacy of his room and enjoy a meal before getting into the conversation he knows they need to have.

"What would you like for dinner?" he asks without looking up. His fingers trail their way down the menu before stopping at Charlotte's usual. "Why am I even asking? You love the Bucatini Arrabbiata."

He chuckles as he finally looks up from the menu, but the laugh catches in his throat.

Charlotte has slipped out of her coat to reveal lingerie, her eyes, speaking to him without words, pulling him in.

"I'm hungry for something *off* the menu, Chase," she says in that deliberately lazy tone as she slowly walks toward him.

"Oh," he whispers. *Oh no.*

Chase licks his lips when she stands so close to him. Her eyes have a sultry look, telling him her intentions are *anything but pure.*

"Charlotte, I thought..." he swallows. "We need—"

Charlotte stands on her tiptoes and presses her lips to Chase's neck. The kiss is slow, deliberate, and authentic, and when it lands on his exposed neck, he thinks not of Willow but of Charlotte. He'd nearly forgotten the feel of her lips on his skin.

She stops kissing him but stands so close to him that he can hear the sound of her heartbeat. She leans her head against his chest, so she can surely hear the rapid staccato of his own heartbeat. She pinches the fabric of his sweater between her fingers. "You know how much I love you in cashmere, Darling, but right now, I need you to take this off."

She doesn't wait for an answer. She doesn't notice his slightly embarrassed wince at the mention of the cashmere, a harbinger, Chase now realizes, of how his evening had been destined to turn out, with him wrapped in a confusing tangle of the two women he couldn't get over.

Charlotte lifts herself and presses her lips against his. It's just like her to take what she wants. The kiss is so much different from before. This time around, she kisses with urgency, like there's not enough time but oh so much to do.

Her kiss is ravenous and, as it drags on, the words in his head diffuse into white noise. Her velvety touch consumes him and he soon forgets everything else that isn't Charlotte.

"Willow, open up!" Lina's voice is loud and intrusive; she's knocking on Willow's door like a police officer serving a warrant.

When Willow opens the door, she finds a visibly shaken, inexplicably furious, Lina. She stomps into the room just as Willow closes the door and turns to her, eyes wide with disbelief.

"What's wrong?" Willow asks.

Lina rubs her palm together. "Chase! I know who he's engaged to!"

"What?"

Lina tries again. "I saw them! Oh my God. Willow...we know her."

Willow doesn't try to guess. She doesn't feel like surprises, but Lina's frantic explanation piques her curiosity. "Okay. So? His fiancée? Who is she?"

"Charlotte Wright, our client..."

9

Answers in the Darkest Hour

Ten years ago...

CHASE TRUDGED DOWN THE ROAD to Willow's house until he found himself on the winding cobblestone pathway, flanked on either side by freshly mown grass leading to a waist-high stone fence fitted with lamp lights, small electric facsimiles of old Victorian street lamps. Chase recalled when Willow had told him she imagined the lights were a million dancing fireflies. He remembered how full of love, how very happy he had been in that moment, listening with rapt attention to the joy she could take in the simplest things, marveling at her ability to share that feeling with him. There, in that moment, he had also seen a million fireflies just as she had seen them. The lights offered him no such comfort now. Their soft yellow illumination now felt as cold and empty as the dismal glow of a winter sun on a cloudy day.

Up ahead, through the entryway in the fence, Chase eyed her family home, a cozy two story Colonial Tudor affair framed by stately elms. Perhaps she was home. He'd been trying to call her for days since the proposal, but she'd refused all of his calls. Somehow, reaching her here might be best for both of them because, in a way, Chase feels betrayed by her.

Walking through the gate and up the small set of stairs leading to the porch and the front door, he rang the doorbell and waited, praying she'll at least want to see him. The door creaked open, hesitantly in the still of the late evening hour, revealing Adam, Willow's younger brother.

"Chase?" he called out, perplexed.

"Is she here?" Chase pleaded, disregarding courtesy, politeness, and everything else for the sake of this question, for a chance to understand why, after so long together, she'd reject him, leave him without any explanation, and not answer his calls.

Adam sighs. "She left for New York this morning."

"Shit," Chase whispered under his breath. He'd already suspected she'd leave, but hearing that she'd actually made the choice to do so makes him both angry and sad.

"What happened?" Adam asks.

Chase runs a hand through his hair and says, "I proposed, Adam. I proposed, and she ran away. And now she won't take my calls."

Adam said nothing, the shock of this news written plainly on his face. He would have expected this kind of irresponsible recklessness from Brynn, Willow's twin sister, but not Willow herself.

"Did she say anything to you?" Chase asked in part because he was curious about what she's told her family, but mostly because he was desperate for some kind of clue, some kind of a lifeline. He was clutching at straws, and he knew it. But even so. *If there's still a chance…*

Adam rubbed the back of his neck and groaned. He liked Chase, he really did, but he hadn't enjoyed being woken up to deal with his sister's heartbroken, confused ex, especially since he had no idea what he could do or say to improve the situation. "Just that you two broke up. I'm sorry, man," he said. He hesitated for a moment, then added, "Do you want me to call her for you?"

Chase wanted to speak to her, to ask her why she'd left; he wanted to hear her voice again, that voice which still gave him butterflies, but he didn't want to risk pushing her further away with a cheap trick like this one.

She'll return, he thought, if he could hold on just for a little while. *This isn't the first time she's run away*, he reminded himself. It had happened once before, back when they were still lovers and he'd told her he loved her. He couldn't find her for days afterward, but he had been patient, and she'd come back and told him she loved him too. Chase knew that if he waited this out, she'd come back again.

So he declined Adam's offer, shaking his head. "No, forget about it," he said. "She'll call me, I know it. I just need to be patient. I'll see you around, Adam."

Chase wakes up from the dream. For the past decade, Chase has recalled that moment again and again when he'd decided to wait for Willow, and she hadn't called or returned.

Beside him, Charlotte stirs, but her eyes remain closed. It's late, hours past midnight.

The memory of the kiss with Willow earlier in the afternoon comes to the forefront of his thoughts, like a cold reminder of his cowardice. This is immediately followed by guilt, which creeps in when he glances down at his beautiful sleeping fiancée.

Sleep refuses to greet him. He knows he doesn't deserve its peaceful embrace, though. His moment of infidelity to Charlotte has made him unrecognizable to himself. *Who are you, man? What the hell are you doing?*

He slips out of bed and tiptoes to the window—his body trembling with the repressed anger that follows the guilt he feels over thinking about Willow while his fiancée sleeps in his bed. Still, despite this, Chase is powerless before his desire to see Willow. She is the answer to a question that has lingered within him for a decade, metastasizing like a malignant tumor, consuming him.

Slipping a t-shirt over his torso, he quietly reaches the door and pulls it open slowly so as not to wake up Charlotte. As wrong as this might be, Chase knows this is his only chance to get the answer he yearns for.

Chase begins to have second thoughts as he approaches her door in the dimly lit hall. Of course, she might be asleep or annoyed by the disturbance. And what about Charlotte? What if she were to find out as well?

I can't turn back now. I've come this far; I have to see this through. Willow's made a hole in my heart; it will only heal if I get answers.

At her door, he knocks. There is no reply, so he repeats it. *See this through.*

Behind the door, Willow lifts herself from underneath the heavy duvet. Sleep is proving to be evasive. So instead, she's been drowning in guilt, replaying the kiss she shared with Chase.

If it had been just a simple, forgettable kiss, she'd have been able to let it go, but it wasn't, and she knew it. His kiss was a promise, assuring her that he still loved her, a craving deep within him for a time they had once shared, and Willow knew she wanted him too.

In retrospect, she shouldn't have done that because now everything has gotten more complicated. She didn't just kiss an old boyfriend she still held a candle for. No, she'd kissed her client's fiancé. She'd confessed her feelings to him.

The knock comes again.

She swallows as she heads to the door. She has only one person in mind who could possibly be behind the door since it is too early to expect visitors, but once she pulls the door open, it's Chase who stands there, his eyes so direct and sad that she feels trapped.

"Chase?"

"Willow, we need to ta—" Two steps in, two steps toward her, and he stops in his tracks as suddenly as if he's hit an invisible wall. His words seize in his throat as his eyes take in her figure.

Her pajama set is revealing, and Chase knows he has to look away, but doing so might ruin the moment. She is still beautiful with her messy hair, her tired but curious eyes, and *silky pink pajamas*...

At that moment, Chase imagines what her lips will taste like, what touching her will feel like.

Oh, fuck me!

She licks her lips and says, "Um, what are you doing here, Chase?"

He is gawking. He knows he is. But it isn't his fault, right? *Right?*

Dear God, is she trying to kill me?

Willow dips her head low, avoiding his eyes. She tucks some hair behind her ear and scratches her neck. "Sorry, I wasn't expecting anyone to be in my room; otherwise, I would have packed some different pajamas."

"Your pajamas..." he begins, but she immediately stops him.

"What are you doing here?"

Right! He clears his throat. "I'm here for answers."

"Answers?" She sounds distressed and even more so by his presence late into the night.

"Yes," he whispers as his head clears. The lust has subsided, and the anger is back. "Answers are why I am here."

"Wouldn't you prefer this wait until morning?" she wraps a slender arm over her body and sighs.

"No. I've lost enough sleep thinking about it." *And my fiancée will likely want brunch.*

She nods as she steps back, beckoning him further into the room. "Why don't you take a seat?"

Moving past her, he sits on the foot of the bed. The duvet is rumpled, the sheets likely still warm from her body. He shakes his head, pushing the image of her sleeping out of his mind.

Willow stands at the closed door, her back to him. When she turns around to look at him, he sees a different side of her: calm and calculating, the side he'd seen when she'd left him hanging ten years ago.

"What would you like to know?" she asks.

There's no time for hesitation. This time around, Chase is confident. "The only thing I've wanted to know since you left me with a ring in my hands."

She swallows.

He watches her under the room's low lighting and marvels at his own audacity. "Why did you say no?"

Willow straightens up, squaring her shoulders, and finally meets his gaze. The time has come; there's nowhere else for her to hide.

Ten years ago...

Willow's twin sister, Brynn, raised a hand to show off her new tattoo.

"It'll wash off," she said as if it mattered. "But I wanted to show you first. What do you think, huh?"

Willow held her hand and twisted the tattoo under the light. For a while, she stared at the image of a dolphin, and then Chase's face swam up before her in its place: his lopsided grin and then, the tears in his eyes after she rejected his proposal. Without thinking, she began to cry.

"Geez, is it really that bad?" Brynn asked playfully, taking Willow's sobs for sarcastic pantomime. But her humor quickly faded when she noticed that Willow's tears were real. "What happened?"

"I left..." she swallows with tear-filled eyes. "I left Chase."

Brynn didn't ask why. She simply pulled Willow in for a hug and rubbed her shoulders gently, slowly, afraid to ask for more.

"Oh, Willow..." she whispered tentatively. "I've got you, sis. I'm here."

In her arms, Willow continued to weep. It was only much later when she was calmer and curled up on the floor, that Brynn decided to ask her the most obvious question. "Why did you leave?"

Willow sniffs and answers. "He proposed."

"What?" Willow said nothing for the longest time, but since she was no longer crying, Brynn didn't push her. Still, the unspoken question hung in the air, refusing to be exercised until it was named. Brynn steeled herself and asked, delicately, "Isn't that a good thing?"

"I couldn't do it, Brynn," she said. "I couldn't—"

"Shh..." Brynn curled up on the floor by her side and linked her fingers with Willow's. "It's alright, Willow. It's alright."

Willow's voice was strangled and desperate. "No, it's not! I just ripped his heart out. I just—"

"Willow..."

Willow swallowed and whispered, "I love him so fucking much, Brynn. But I can't marry him. Because I—"

She stopped talking and closed her eyes. Beside her, Brynn said, "Willow, it's alright. It'll be alright."

And Willow wanted to believe that, wanted it to be true with every fiber of her being, but she knew in her heart that it was too late.

Willow swallows, thinking back to that moment with Brynn and how much hurt she'd felt. She knits her fingers together and clears her throat.

"I wasn't ready, Chase," she says, and with more fervor, she adds, "I wasn't ready to get married. We were just so young. You were all I ever knew."

Chase pushes himself off the bed. The way he stands, almost towering over Willow with a face full of hurt indignation, makes her feel small.

"Is that such a bad thing?" he asks, his voice soft compared to his stern expression.

She says the first thing that comes to mind. "Honestly, it is, yes."

He frowns. "What do you mean, yes?"

"I mean…we were together for two years, Chase," she says, rolling her eyes. "We started dating as soon as I moved to Portland. I didn't even give myself a chance to settle in before I jumped into a relationship with you. You were my first everything."

Chase takes a staggering step forward, almost bowled over by the weight of his emotions. "You were my first too. Is it so wrong that I also wanted you to be my last?"

"No, that's not what I'm saying," she runs a shaky hand through her hair and wills herself not to cry. "I wanted you to be my last as well, Chase."

He pushes his hands down against his sides and eyes her. "Yes, your rejection made that *abundantly clear*."

She moves closer to him, her anger now the reflection of his. "Do you think I wasn't a mess? Do you think I left you and just…just moved on with my life like we meant nothing? Because that was the hardest thing I ever had to do, Chase."

Her eyes are the saddest he's ever seen them. And while he doubts what she says, he doesn't interrupt her; his curiosity is too intense. He needs to hear this.

"But I'm glad I did it," she continues. "I found myself, Chase. I left you because I needed to know that I didn't lose myself in loving you."

"You thought you lost yourself by dating me?"

This isn't the answer he's been expecting, but it's enough for him because now he's sure that being with him meant absolutely nothing to her.

"No, it's not exactly like that. Chase, listen…" she says, her voice insistent.

But Chase doesn't want to listen anymore. Hearing how she feels hurts him, but more importantly, he realizes he doesn't want to relive the past again, not the one where he's both powerless and heartbroken.

He starts for the door, but Willow is quick, and, before he reaches for the doorknob, her fingers grab his arm. He stops and looks down at her fingers, seeing the paleness of her palm, and immediately feels the need to kiss her fingers one at a time.

Why can't I let her go? he asks himself. After her confession tonight, how could his heart still long for her?

"It was never your fault, Chase," she whispers.

Willow's grip is light and easy to walk away from, but her timid fingers and throaty whisper are enough for him to read the plea. She is asking him to stay, and although he wants this situation to mean something, anything, else, he is sure she feels the same overpowering craving as him.

Her touch is seemingly innocent, but the tension between them grows as her hands linger. Chase begins to remember every memory they'd once shared, and, as they come flooding back, he realizes that they are stepping into dangerous territory. Even so he isn't sure he wants to step out of it just yet.

He hears her sharp intake of breath and sees the terseness in her lips. She begins to trail her fingers upward through the length of his arm. He shivers from her touch, and goose bumps rise where her finger grazes.

"Willow…" he startles himself with her name. It settles in the space between them.

"I'm sorry, Chase," she says, pulling her hands away.

He turns to her now; concern etched across his face. "What was it then?"

"What was what?" She doesn't look him in the eye when she asks this.

"What made you leave if it wasn't me?"

"Myself," Willow answers quickly. "I was scared that getting engaged so young would change my goals. I had so much I wanted to do before settling down with you. I figured I wouldn't be able to accomplish it if we got married right away. So I left."

Chase holds his breath, silent.

She continues, "I knew I wouldn't pursue my dreams if I stayed with you. And it wasn't because I thought you would make me. It's because I knew I would forget about my plans."

This time around, he finds his voice. Willow's reasons for leaving make no sense to him, no matter how hard he tries to defend it, but he truly wants to understand her. "What…what do you mean?"

"I was so dependent on you, Chase," she responds. "Our years together made me forget that I was my own person. I realized that I had lost myself—lost my way. I didn't want to become that girl. I didn't want to be the sort of person with dreams and career goals who just throws them away for love. And I know how brutal that sounds now, but back then, it was all I felt. So when you got down on one knee and proposed—I couldn't say yes."

Chase doesn't say anything for the longest time, but his eyes are deadly serious, and when she stares up at him, she sees that he looks almost distant, remote.

Please, God, tell me he doesn't hate me more…

"Why didn't you tell me?"

"I thought you would be angry."

"So you thought leaving me, without a word, right after I asked to be forever yours was better than explaining why you weren't ready? You thought that *that* wouldn't make me angry?"

"I was so young, Chase, and still so immature. I didn't think to talk it out with you."

Chase comes closer and uses his fingers to lift her chin. "I wish you would have told me," he says softly, his voice full of longing and regret. "Things could have been so different."

"Chase…"

119

"It's true, Willow."

She nods, and a lock of hair slips across her face. Chase pushes it back behind her ear with a rueful smile. But Willow isn't smiling. In truth, she feels like crying, like burying herself in his arms and crying and apologizing, even though she wants to continue to pretend that she's strong.

Her voice is low and rough when she speaks. "It's my only regret."

He drags his breath and pushes his forehead against hers. Willow feels so small now with Chase so close. The weight of her confession snags at both of their hearts now, dragging them down together.

"Thank you for telling me, Willow," he says to her. "It's haunted me for such a long time."

She nods.

Chase steps away from her when, suddenly and to her surprise, she feels bereft of all emotion.

"I should get going," Chase says, "it's already three."

Willow wonders what it would be like if she asked him to stay or if he'd even want to. She nearly asks him before changing her mind. "Alright."

He turns around at the door. Willow stands close to him as though she doesn't want him to go. Her lingering gaze is almost enough to drive him over the edge. This might just be their final moment together and Chase doesn't want it to end with a simple goodbye. So, he waits.

He thinks about tracing her jawline, kissing her full, waiting lips. Her eyes are the color of midnight in the semi-darkness of the room, but he can see a reflection of his own desire in those eyes. He thinks a kiss is an innocent farewell, or at least it can be, but this is a lie he's telling himself to validate his want.

"Do you feel like your entire existence is being tested right now? Like you're being pulled into two different directions, and you're unsure which one is right?" Chase swallows.

She says nothing.

"Because that's how I feel," he confesses. "I'm torn between what I have and what I want."

She runs a hand through her hair again and lets out the breath she's been holding. It comes out as a tremor that weakens her the moment it leaves her lips. "And what is it that you want, Chase?" she says, tired but also defiant.

Willow is daring him. It's not something she'd normally do, but she stops thinking and acts instinctively in the face of naked passion. Slowly, she raises a hand and places it on his chest. He can see the want in her face as she stares him down from his eyes to the bridge of his nose and then on his lips.

"Chase, I want—"

Her voice catches in her throat as his deep eyes bore deep into her, creating mounting pressure through her entire frame. He has a slight smile etched on his lips. It's those lips she'd spent two years exploring, lips she'd kissed less than twelve hours ago.

Then, she remembers that he has someone else. She pulls her hand from his chest and whispers, "We can't."

Slowly he pulls away. "You're right," he agrees dubiously, like he doesn't know for sure. "Goodbye, Willow Harris."

And then he leaves, and she is once again alone. "Goodbye, Chase Kennedy," she whispers to the empty room.

10

The Significance of You

CHASE GRABS A HAND TOWEL from the holder and wipes the fog off the bathroom mirror. Alone, he studies his frenzied expression in the reflection. He wonders what others see when they look at him. Can they see the sadness in his eyes that never fully seems to disappear? Chase lifts his chin and brushes his thumb across the faint scar, just as Willow had done yesterday. He feels bad for brushing it off when she mentioned it, but the story behind it isn't something he wanted to share with her. In truth, it was the result of a fall during a drunken night out back when he first moved to Chicago. He had to get two stitches and is now forever reminded of the mess he used to be.

I'm still a mess, he thinks to himself, knowing that, in the span of thirty-six hours, he'd met his first love again and said his goodbyes as well.

He knows he's crossed an emotional line by convincing her to spend the day with him, putting himself in the position to be unfaithful to his fiancée. He knows there will be no reconciliation when he's selfishly kissed another woman in the heat of the moment, but last night had taught him something important: he can not continue the engagement.

It isn't because of Willow, although he'd only be lying to himself if he claimed her coming back isn't part of the reason, but it's more than that. Chase doesn't feel the spark anymore and indeed has not for some time. His relationship with Charlotte had been broken long before Willow walked back into his life, and, for the happiness of everyone involved, Chase believes this is the only way.

Once he walks back into the room, he's startled by Charlotte still in bed, the sheets wrapped around her.

"Oh! I didn't realize you were still here."

She sits upright and groans. Chase watches her curiously, surprised that she hasn't taken off yet. It's become her usual MO since the engagement: absconding before the first rays of the morning sun, leaving only a note behind. Chase realizes now, by watching her, that he's been the one waiting every single time.

"You're usually long gone by now."

"I thought we could do brunch," she responds, smiling coyly, lifting a finger in his direction. "I don't know about you, but I worked up quite the appetite last night."

I guess this morning is as good as any, Chase decides. *But I'll wait until after brunch; no need to ruin her favorite meal.*

"Sure, Char," he says. "Just let me get dressed."

While he dresses, she excuses herself and slips into the washroom. When she comes back again, she is already dressed in her signature green coat and a white dress.

"Shall we?"

The lobby's bright lights greet them once they exit the elevator. Hand in hand, Chase walks with Charlotte, their feet patterned to adjust to the extravagant marble of the place. She falls into step with him, so comfortable in the hotel environment that it's as though she belongs here, and Chase begins to forget they have a life outside of this hotel.

Charlotte also speaks casually, like there is enough time to say whatever they want. "I was thinking we could go to that little café you love."

He thinks she's unusually kind and attentive this morning, but he likes the effort, likes that she's here and wants to do the little things with him. *And where has this woman been hiding all year?*

"That sounds great, Char," he says. "I'm glad we can have some time together..."

She pauses, her lips curling into a saucy smirk. "We just spent the entire night together, Darling..."

The memories come flooding back, and he thinks instead about Willow in her pajamas, the softness of her skin, and how she looked at him like she wanted all of him.

He sighs, "Actually, Char, I wanted to—"

She pulls her hands away, looking in the other direction. "Oh, my God!" she yelps. "My wedding dress designer is here! Come on; I want to introduce you two!"

Charlotte doesn't wait for him to answer as she dashes off in the direction she's pointing. He can tell that she's very excited, but more than that, he supposes there is a kind of appeal in meeting the designer of her wedding dress here.

"Alright, but only for a moment," Chase calls out and then begins walking in her direction. "Where is—"

He stops, frowning. There, in front of him, he finds Willow and her friend from yesterday, and from here on, he realizes something fundamental: secrets, like patiently vengeful ghosts, always come back to haunt you in the end, no matter how long they have to wait.

You've got to be kidding me.

He walks over to where the three women are now perched, and Charlotte links her arm to his again. "Oh, Chase," she says, smiling widely. "Ladies, this is my fiancé, Chase Kennedy. Chase, Darling, this is Lina Rose. And this is my designer, Willow Harris."

Chase knows he needs to be careful with his reaction to this introduction. He can neither run and hide nor stay silent, so he stretches out his hand, first to Lina and then to the woman he'd kissed only hours before. "It's nice to meet you both."

"It's nice to meet you too, Mr. Kennedy," Willow says, politely but without much visible interest.

Mr. Kennedy.

It shouldn't bother him, but it does. He says nothing as his eyes narrow, studying her closely. Willow avoids eye contact and flinches when Lina taps her shoulders. "Hey, Willow?" Lina says.

"Yes?"

"Weren't you just telling me about needing the groom's opinion for that surprise?"

Willow is startled by the urgency in her tone, but more than that, she knows there is no surprise. "What surprise?"

Lina nudges Willow and raises her brows. "You know, for the *bride*?"

127

Catching on, Willow gives Lina a knowing glance and smiles at Charlotte, her eyes searching. "Do you mind if I borrow the groom for a few minutes?"

Charlotte lets go of his arm and clasps her wrists. "Of course not!" she exclaims, her voice rising an octave in excitement. "You can take him all day if you want! I love surprises!"

Willow leans back on her heels, and Charlotte turns back to Chase. "You don't mind, do you, Darling?"

Chase glares at Willow and then crosses his arm. "Not at all."

"Brilliant!" Charlotte says, turning back around.

Lina says, "Great! Charlotte, would you like to see some of the sketches Willow's put together?"

"Yes, please!" Charlotte says, following Lina away.

Alone, Chase leans in and catches a whiff of her smell. *God, she smells delightful.* "Really, with the 'Mr. Kennedy,' Willow?"

She shrugs.

"Are you trying to get a rise out of me?" he says, doubtful. "You know how I feel when you say that."

She arches an eyebrow when she speaks, the kind that makes her nearly unrecognizable. "Why didn't you tell me Charlotte Wright is your fiancée?"

"I didn't think it was relevant."

"Of course it's relevant," she snaps.

"First of all, how was I supposed to know that you knew her?"

"You didn't know I was her dress designer?"

"We're not really—" he swallows. He feels embarrassed to admit this to Willow. "Our communication hasn't been that great lately."

Willow rolls her eyes and responds flatly, "Wonderful."

Chase frowns. Her expression, he's seen it before. "Wait, why the hell are *you* mad?"

She sighs and glances down at the floor. Her voice is a whisper. "I'm not mad at you. Not really. It's just that—well, I'm upset that you're engaged—and not to me."

When Willow's eyes shoot upward, the feeling of holding her in his arms becomes all too powerful and demanding for Chase. Her words slice through his heart like dagger wounds, but he lets her speak.

She continues, getting lost in her tangent, "Of course, you're engaged to my client. This is karma! The universe is paying me back for leaving you the way I did. I can't be—"

"Willow," he calls gently.

"What?"

There is a hint of a smile when he speaks. "You're upset because I'm not engaged to you?"

"Chase, you're engaged to my client," Willow says in a low, controlled voice. "This adds another layer of complications that I'm sure you haven't even thought of. Yet, you're hung up on this?"

"Okay, I'm sorry," he says, raising his hands in defense. "But for the record, Willow? You and I could've been married by now."

Willow clears her throat, and the silence becomes awkward.

"I wish we were engaged too," he says, sighing deeply.

Willow's chin quivers, and she bites her lip. "Don't say something you don't mean, Chase."

"I do mean it."

"You're making this harder than it already is," she pushes back, her voice wavering slightly now. "We agreed after last night that—"

"Willow," Chase whispers. He glances over her shoulder to where Lina and Charlotte are seated. Char's back is to them, so he reaches for Willow's arm, gently grasping it.

She holds her breath; her metallic gaze frantically searches his. "Are you insane? She's right there."

Reluctantly, he releases her arm and runs a hand through his hair. "I'm sorry, I just—"

I can't resist you.

"It's fine," she says coldly.

Chase sighs, allowing the moment to pass. "Um, so is there actually a surprise?"

"No, that's just Lina giving us an excuse to talk." Willow visibly relaxes with the change in subject.

Chase laughs, surprised, and she smiles. "I already like her."

"I don't know where I'd be without her," Willow replies, smiling gently.

She takes a deep breath and meets his gaze. He thinks that, paired with her dark brown hair, her eyes look pale under the lobby's lighting.

"Your fiancée is really great, Chase." There's sorrow in her voice. "I—I'm happy for you."

Chase knits his eyebrows together. "Are you, though?"

Willow sucks in a sharp breath, nodding her head. "You've found someone who—well, she loves you, Chase."

"What if she didn't?"

"She does, though," Willow responds. Chase can see the pain she's in. "You should've heard the way she spoke about you at the meeting yesterday. All I've ever wanted was for you to find someone who loves you like that. Who loves you in…"

Her voice trails off, and now it's Chase's turn to suck in a sharp breath.

"Who loves me in the way you can't."

"No, that's not—"

"Go ahead, Willow, you can say it. I can handle it," Chase pushes bitterly. "I mean, it's not like it comes as a surprise."

"Chase—"

"God, this isn't fair, is it?"

"What do you mean?"

Chase hesitates, only for a moment, debating if he wants to cross this line. Finally, he decides he's already crossed dozens of lines over the past few days. "Would you still choose me, Willow? If given a chance, right here, right now, would you still choose me?"

"You're not asking me this here."

"I am asking you this here."

Willow sighs and runs a hand through her hair. "She's my client, Chase."

"Don't focus on that."

"Then what should I focus on, hm?"

"Yourself," Chase responds. "Forget everything and everyone else. Don't think about the possible repercussions, don't think about the circumstances that brought us both here at the same time. None of it matters—"

"It matters, Chase; it has to matter," she whispers. "Because if it didn't, then what the hell are we doing? What the hell *have we been doing?*"

"What would you choose, Willow," he insists, "if the opportunity was there?"

"You."

It's one simple word, yet it holds immense significance. It may hold the key to a whole new future, and Willow's released it into the world. She exhales a small sigh of relief, and Chase rolls his shoulders back, feeling twice as tall and on top of the world.

"I've got to go," he finally says. Willow's face drops. "Take care, Willow."

Without another word, Chase side steps around her and makes his way over to Charlotte and Lina, leaving Willow spiraling.

11

Absolve Me

Four years ago...

"WHEN YOU SAID THE RIVERWALK would be dead right now, part of me didn't believe you," Charlotte cried out ecstatically.

"Do you really think anyone else would be out here at this hour, especially after the downpour we just had?" Chase asks.

"I can't believe *I'm* out here at this hour after such a heavy downpour," she replied, teasing him.

"And I can't believe you actually sat on these wet steps with me."

Chase wanted to laugh at the absurdity of this, but when she faced him, he was overwhelmed by her beauty. Her auburn locks, wet from the rain, were plastered to her face. She pursed her lips, seeming to search for something to say. Chase waited thinking only of her as they sat on the wet steps.

"There are few people in this world I would do this for, Darling," she said matter-of-factly.

"Oh, I know," he laughed. "I'm glad I made the cut."

She laughed with him, delighted by the conversation and, most of all, by the company beside her. And for a while, neither of them spoke, enjoying the comfortable silence, so much so that Chase realized how long it'd been since he'd last felt like this with someone.

Then she asked, "Chase?"

"Yes, Char?" He turned to her, offering a smile but dropped it when his eyes met the solemnity in her gaze. "What is it?"

"Will you tell me about her?"

Chase paused. This was a conversation they hadn't had yet, and hearing the question spill from her lips without warning stunned him. He watched her for a reaction, but Charlotte was calm and focused.

She turned away from him, watching the stately cadence of the river, but he saw through her. When she bit down on her lower lip, he knew she was a nervous wreck for having dared to ask the forbidden question.

"Her?" he asked simply, offering her an out.

But Charlotte didn't take it. Instead, she nodded, keeping her eyes fixed on the waterway before them.

"Someone hurt you in the past, Darling. You've done well hiding the rather large hole in your heart, but I know you well enough now to see it."

Receiving no response from Chase, she turned towards him, struggling to control the tempest of her emotions. Her voice quavered. "I left someone behind in London."

He'd known snippets of her past life but had avoided asking about it. Chase had always walked delicately around the subject, but now, she wanted to tell him everything, baring herself to him, and he suddenly felt an overwhelming pressure building inside of him.

"Declan Williams," she breathed, her voice a barely audible susurrus in the damp evening air. "I've known him since I was quite young; we grew up together. He's the first person I ever fell in love with. We were together for a few years, but we ended our romantic relationship when I decided to study here in Chicago. We were too young for that kind of long-distance commitment."

Chase turned away from her and shuffled his feet, suddenly as uncomfortable in that instant as he had been happy just moments before. Her words, her confession, brought back memories that he would rather have kept buried, so close were the parallels of their respective heartbreaks.

"He was a huge part of my life, and I know part of me will always hold some love for him," she continued. "Sometimes you give a piece of yourself to another and know you'll never get it back. But you can't let that stop you from sharing pieces of yourself with others. That's the whole point of life, isn't it? To experience as much as possible with the time you've been given?"

As Charlotte gazed into Chase's eyes, her own filled with a sense of wonder and anticipation. Her brows furrowed, emphasizing her eagerness to open up and share a piece of her soul with him.

Chase suspected that this is something not many people were ever privileged to see, the vibrant beating heart beneath the oh so carefully maintained facade of cool, collected poise, and he can't help but feel a sense of longing; the time they'd spent together had felt so fleeting compared to the seemingly interminable years he'd spent searching for his own lost soul. *No*, he thought. That wasn't quite right. His soul hadn't been lost. It'd been stolen.

"Six years ago, I proposed to the woman I thought I'd spend the rest of my life with." Charlotte was right. She'd known she was. Her words opened him up, allowing him to see things from a new perspective or at least to talk about them with someone who really understood the hurt. Misery loved company, so there they were, vulnerable and miserable together. But this was, Charlotte had thought, a necessary hurdle for Chase to get over if he was really going to be with her, to really love her. Oh, she'd known that Chase liked her, but she wasn't interested in being *liked* or even *really liked;* she wanted to be *loved.* And it looked like the path from like to love was taking them over a mountain of misery and, hopefully, into a valley of catharsis where they could both heal and love each other.

Chase stared into the middle distance thoughtfully, measuring his response, weighing his words very carefully. Willow's abandonment had left him scarred, but the hurt had become easier to deal with when Charlotte was there. He'd always been hesitant to let anyone in, let anyone see the sort of man he'd become for fear of rejection, but with Charlotte, Chase thinks about trying, about wanting and needing and staying.

And so, on the cold steps in front of the river, Chase opened his heart to Charlotte Wright.

In the café, Chase begins to feel excruciatingly alone. Charlotte sits across from him, and in a few months, she'll be his wife, but the loneliness feels like a weight pressing down on his chest, a weight that might kill him if he isn't careful.

It's not because of the sudden and unexpected emotional connection with his past love or the fact that there's a sharp contrast between him and Charlotte. Although, there are times when Chase wants to put that uncomfortable fact into focus and really examine it. But the real issue is in how distant she gets even when they're together. Today, Charlotte is on her phone, her hands tapping furiously, her eyes focused.

"Char?" he calls.

She does not look up at him but arches an eyebrow to indicate that he has been heard.

He asks, "Can you look at me when I talk to you?"

She pauses momentarily, apparently startled. "I'm just replying to some messages. What's the big deal?"

He leans back against the booth. "You've been on your phone since we sat down, and that was an hour ago."

She taps her nails on the table, frowning. "Sorry for having important messages to attend to," she says, delivering the mother of all non-apologies.

It's just like her to be so *inconsiderate*. The weight comes down again, so fiercely this time that Chase begins to feel faint. He wants to leave, but can he? Should he?

"Charlotte…" he begins.

"What?"

"Can we get out of here?" he asks. "Take a walk? I need to talk to you in private."

Finally, she meets his gaze. "Is everything alright, Darling?"

Chase stops moving, stops nervously shuffling his feet underneath the table so he can have a good look at her. The quick change in the tone of her voice is very nearly frightening, but he's gotten used to it since the proposal. But did he *want* to be used to it? A person could get *used* to being in prison, but that didn't make it an ideal arrangement.

She's changed, he thinks, but it isn't just the quick change from short and frustrated to sweet and concerned. It's how cut off and out of sorts he feels with her when she used to be so warm and full of love. Now, he sees the change becoming more and more evident each time he visits her because it is very apparent how little she desires to spend time with him.

Chase has never been the sort of person to give up on love or, at least, a promising relationship. It isn't an obsessive want but rather an enthusiastic thirst for happiness. It's why he continues to pursue her, grasping at the slight, unraveling threads of their relationship.

Today, Chase realizes that he is far too exhausted for such games. Just too damn tired. He wants out.

"No, Charlotte, everything is not okay," he says, rising from the booth and placing cash on the table. "Please, let's take a walk."

Reluctantly, she pulls herself from their booth and follows him outside.

The sky is overcast and dull, but the tension between them blazes vividly.

Charlotte flexes her hands but releases them and sighs. "What's going on, Darling?"

It is a pet name that she'd given him without a second thought on the first night they met; the word used to ignite a fire in him, but hearing it now makes him cringe and leaves him feeling cold, the flames burning down to ashes. It's probably because he can tell she doesn't really mean it, at least not how she used to, and this counterfeit emotion, a cheap one at that, flips a switch in his head.

He says, "I want to talk to you about our engagement."

She pauses, and Chase stops with her, coming to a standstill in front of her. There's no going back now; he knows it.

"What about it?" she asks, concerned, a mixture of worry and annoyance in the question.

Chase lets out the breath he's been holding all night, possibly even all year. "I just feel like things have been…off for a while. A long while, actually."

He pauses, curious to see if she'll interject, but she doesn't. It hurts him that she doesn't, but he carries on.

"I don't believe we love one another the way an engaged couple is supposed to. We can't enter a lifelong commitment if we can hardly stand to look at each other."

Her expression doesn't change. It's almost like she's been half-expecting this conversation. Her eyes search Chase's, but there are no strained emotions or longing looks. She pinches her arm, a tick he knows she does only when nervous.

He continues, "It takes two to get to this point, and I'll own up to my mistakes. I know we planned that I'd visit more than I have. My partnership at the firm was fairly new when you moved, but I had enough freedom to insist on visiting you more. I didn't though. I didn't insist on it, and I truly am sorry for that."

Still, she says nothing, but her eyes lower to his arm to see how it nervously flexes beneath his coat. The silence grows into painful awkwardness, yet still, she doesn't respond.

Chase tries again to get more...hell, to get *anything* from her. "But all we seem to do is fight. The only time we're not fighting is when we're—"

She looks at him again, and he sees the sadness in her eyes.

"This isn't working anymore, Charlotte," he says. "And I think that's okay."

She bites down hard on her lower lip and sniffs. Chase wonders if she'll run, he prays that she won't, not until they've both agreed to walk away.

"Char," he says softly, reaching for her arm, "*please…* say something."

"I'm…I'm having an affair!" she blurts out.

Chase pulls his arm away as though her touch burns him. He takes a few steps back, stumbling, a strange sensation of vertigo overtaking him. He frowns and, for a while, remains silent, dumbstruck.

No matter how hard he wills the words to come, they just won't. The idea that Charlotte might have been having an affair has never crossed his mind, and today, she just spits it out like an afterthought.

She rests her hands on her hips, visibly unsure what to do with them in the moment. Tears pool in her eyes, but he can see more than that; he can see fear, worry, and deep sadness. But for the first time, Chase doesn't need to wrap his arms around her to stop the tears.

Finally, he asks, "You're…You're what?!"

"I'm sorry, Chase, I'm so sorry!"

He wants to take one, two…ten steps away from her until the distance between them feels endless, but her confession keeps him rooted to the spot as surely as if he's been impaled on it. Chase blinks back the tears threatening to fall, but her words feel like they're breaking into him, crawling in through his tear ducts, branching out into his heart and mind until his shoulders sag and his gaze lands softly on his shoes, almost in rebuke of the traitorous feet so completely failing to remove him from this situation.

She's still talking, still trying to explain the reason, but all he can think about is how much time he's spent leading up to this trip, planning to fight for her, longing to reconnect and repair whatever had gone wrong.

The first person he's ever allowed into his heart after Willow's betrayal has been cheating on him, and when his mind mulls this over, he thinks there might be a problem with *him*, not them. After all, what's the x-factor in both situations? *Him.* It makes him think of the adage, 'If you walk into a room and everybody's an asshole, maybe *you're* the asshole.'

It's taken him so long to let himself become vulnerable in front of anyone, and here comes Charlotte, ripping his heart to shreds. A drum-like pounding in his ears keeps him from drowning, but now Chase wants nothing more than to hurt her as much as she's hurt him.

His hands clench into fists and he eyes her balefully, his voice thundering in fury. "How could you?!"

She shivers when she speaks. "The distance..." She sounds uncertain, like an actor who hasn't rehearsed her lines because she didn't think she'd be performing tonight.

"The *distance*? Are you fucking kidding me?!" Chase shouts, repulsed by her excuse and by the fact that she isn't even trying to defend herself in any kind of plausible way. "That's a shitty excuse, and you know it!"

She runs a hand through her hair and groans. "I know! I'm sorry, Chase!"

He shakes his head, vexed in equal measures by her heartless behavior and tactless apologies. "I don't want to hear it, Charlotte! I trusted you"—his voice breaks—"I trusted you."

The tears begin to fall now, and Charlotte makes no move to clean her face up. Rivulets of broken mascara run down her cheeks, but her eyes are on him. For once, he, and no one and nothing else, has her full attention.

Too late, Charlotte, Chase thinks. *You're a day late and a dollar short.*

She takes a step forward but stops, both desperate and afraid. "Chase, please..."

"You know what?" he asks bitterly, his voice laced with malice. "Maybe this is easier. Maybe this absolves me."

"What—what do you mean?"

"I'll post your stuff when I get back to Chicago. But after today, I never want to see you again."

12

The Meaning of Life

WILLOW READ ONCE IN A magazine that the value of true love was defined over time. It made no sense back then, but for the first time, she thinks back to it and imagines that there is some sort of truth in this.

After a decade apart, she reconnects with the love of her life, and this transformation, subtle in its form, makes her both happy and anxious. What if the magazine was right in some way and time apart is enough to make the love even stronger than it already was?

"How are you doing?" Lina asks as she slips into her coat. It's the first time she's brought it up since Chase left with Charlotte earlier in the day.

Willow shrugs the question off. "What's this guy's name again?"

Lina adjusts her coat before shifting her full attention to Willow. She narrows her eyes and studies her friend closely, silently, for a few moments.

"Mmmhmmm…" she says, as though verifying a suspicion. Don't change the topic," she chides, a hint of the reproachful mother in her voice. "What did Chase say to you this morning?"

"It doesn't matter what he said, Lina," Willow responds. "It's done."

"What's done? You and him? He and Charlotte? Our job?" Lina pulls out a tube of red lipstick from her purse and uncaps it. She says, "If we're down a client, you need to let me know."

"We're not down a client," Willow mumbles.

Lina pauses before capping the tube and turning to face her friend again. "I'm worried about you."

"Don't be. Just…focus on your hot date, okay?"

"You know, I'll stay with you in a heartbeat if you need me to. Forget the guy. The world's full of guys. There are literally billions of them," she says, shrugging off the men of the world with a roll of her shoulders and a devil-may-care smile.

Willow knows Lina would happily drop everything for her. Lina is one of the only people she can count on most days—her most consistent relationship. It's lovely but a little sad if she thinks about it for too long.

"You deserve to have some fun," Willow responds dismissively.

Lina crosses the room and kneels next to Willow, who sits cross-legged on the floor, surrounded by sketches of wedding dresses and veils.

"And you deserve the fucking world, Wills. Don't forget that, okay?"

Willow chews her bottom lip, nodding in wordless affirmation. Lina's phone chimes and she sneaks a peek before glancing at the door. Her date is here.

"Have fun tonight, yeah?" Willow nudges her friend and flashes her a ridiculous wink.

Lina scoffs and rolls her eyes as she rises to her feet. "Oh, stop. It's not like I'm looking to fall in love." Right before she opens the door, she looks back at Willow and gives her a cheeky wink. "Don't wait up."

When the door to her room closes with a 'click,' and Willow's finally alone, she releases a deep sigh and leans back against the bed. She's been thinking about Chase non-stop, but she avoids speaking his name out loud for fear that she'll burst into tears.

But now, the tears spring freely from her eyes. The realization that she's truly lost him settles over her like a dark storm cloud. It was foolish of her to admit that she longs to be with him. She knows she should've let things lie as they had when he left her room last night. But seeing him with Charlotte and how he wrapped her up in his arms as they left the lobby made it all too clear that there was nothing left for Willow and Chase.

In a dark corner of her mind, part of her wonders if she should have asked him last night to choose her. Perhaps she could have convinced him; if she'd said something, he could be with her right now.

She glares at the sketches of wedding dresses strewn on the floor around her, wedding dresses that her clients have worn, wedding dresses that her future clients will wear, and, of course, the wedding dress that Charlotte will wear when she marries the love of Willow's life.

"God, Willow, get a grip," she tells herself, aggressively wiping the tears from her cheeks with the heels of her hands. Pushing herself up from the ground, she rises to her feet, deciding that the first step to getting out of this slump is to get out of this room.

"Cheers," Chase lazily raises his glass to the bartender, who offers him a tight-lipped smile in return.

His phone vibrates on the bar beside his glass. Charlotte's name flashes on the screen again, and once more, Chase declines. She's been calling him on and off for the past few hours.

"Let her call," he grumbles before taking a sip. The bitter taste of the Negroni brings comfort to Chase, a beacon of solace in his upended life.

Perhaps he should've seen it coming. Looking back at Charlotte's behavior over the last several months, the affair makes sense. He always assumed their physical distance was the reason for emotional distance, but it appears that was only a contributing factor, a symptom of a more serious problem.

He could debate the reasons behind his poor luck in love all night, but Chase knows it won't do him any good. He'll still end up in the same place he's found himself once again: spiraling. More than a bit drunk now, he thinks about the word 'spiral.' He thinks about how eagles spiral. Eagles cartwheel from great heights, plummeting to the earth in a corkscrew of rapidly accelerating feathers only to soar back up at the last possible minute before a terminal impact with the earth below. It's dangerous. Sometimes, eagles die doing it. That's why it's called a death spiral. But here's the thing, Chase thinks to himself, eagles spiral in pairs. They spiral with their mates.

It's more of a love spiral. And it takes two to spiral. *Jesus, Chase. You can't even do a proper spiral.*

Finishing off his drink with one large gulp, he sets the glass on the bartop a little harder than intended and pushes himself from the stool. He sends the bartender a mock salute and wanders slowly out of the bar and into the lobby of the Wright Hotel.

Sleep it off; start again tomorrow, Chase decides as he steps into the elevator. He's faintly aware of a headache that's beginning to blossom in the back of his head, a sign that, come tomorrow, he'll regret having drank on an empty stomach tonight. Once his finger hits the button for the twelfth floor, he hovers over the button for the eighth. *Willow.*

The doors slide closed just as he presses the golden '8,' better judgment be damned. At this moment, all Chase wants is to see Willow's face. He longs for the comfort that her silvery gaze has always offered. As the elevator climbs higher and higher, he smiles to himself for the first time since this afternoon.

Maybe this is for the best. Maybe—

"Chase?"

He blinks, curious if he's conjured her presence. The doors have opened, revealing the only woman he's been hoping to see. When he notices her frantic gaze, he offers her a calming smile, the sort gentle enough to melt anyone's heart.

"Willow," he whispers.

And because she's at a loss for words, she says the first thing that comes to mind. "Are you going down?"

He lifts his chin in a charmingly roguish way, and she knows he is trying to make her feel comfortable and happy, but she can tell there is something more. The sadness in his eyes is the kind she's seen before. "Join me?"

She steps into the elevator as the doors close and sighs. "I was going to head to the bar downstairs for some wine. Truth be told, I was looking for something to calm my nerves."

Willow sneaks a glance up at Chase, who's watching her closely. His eyes narrow, searching her face like he's trying to memorize every inch. But he remains quiet, so Willow decides to break the silence.

"I feel...weird about this morning. I know it's not my place—I'm probably damned for even thinking this—but I have to ask," she rambles. "Chase, are you—"

"You look so beautiful, Willow," he interrupts softly, his voice just above a whisper and only slightly slurred.

She pauses, caught off guard. His eyes are sad, but his words ring true. She can feel their powerful impact in her heart.

"Thank you," she replies, in a voice just as soft.

In truth, she does look beautiful at that moment, standing by his side, eyes bright, lips parted halfway as though she is on the cusp of saying something. A decade hasn't changed how easily he can read her, and as he continues to stare at her, he can tell that she's been waiting for him all day.

He knows this because he recognizes the look. It's the same one he'd worn waiting for her years ago searching, hoping, and praying she'd come back. Her hair is a little messy, the way it tends to be when she changes her clothes more than once before deciding what to wear, and Chase wants to laugh at this juxtaposition, the crown of unruly ringlets adorning the urgent expression on her face, but he can't.

She's fidgeting, shifting from one foot to another, her jaw clenching and relaxing. It isn't difficult to know that she's biting the inside of her cheek to stop herself from blurting out the question that's been on her mind all day, but Chase is uninterested, not in Willow but in answering her questions—or anyone's for that matter.

There is no answer to give anyway.

Without thinking, Chase steps forward and hits the lift's emergency stop button. For a while, he hesitates, his hand against the button, and he blows hot air out of his lungs. Behind him, Willow's voice swallows the emptiness.

"Are you alright, Chase?" she asks.

He turns back to her and closes the distance between them. He slips his hand in hers, and she doesn't object. Instead, her eyes meet his, and she swallows. It is a challenge—her gaze bearing down hard on his—to finish what he'd started back in the London Eye.

But she doesn't know just how willing he is to step up to the challenge, just how ready he is to take her into his arms and taste her lips.

Chase leans in close until he can feel her breath on his skin. "If I kissed you right now, would you stop me?" His voice is low, throaty, and... *hungry*.

Willow can faintly smell the Campari on his breath, and just for a moment, she wonders if she should lie to him. If she should put her hands on his chest and gently push him away.

But the moment is fleeting.

Her eyes don't stray away from his when she answers. "That depends. Are you free to kiss me?"

He knows why she's asking this, but Chase wants to avoid the truth a little longer. Still, her wide, beautiful eyes and her full, parted lips make him wonder if telling the truth might be better. "I wouldn't ask if I wasn't free, Willow."

She swallows. Chase's eyes travel from her chin down to her throat watching the graceful bob of her throat before rising back to the perfect Cupid's bow of her lips. Her voice is redolent with playful challenge when she asks, "Then what are you waiting for, *Mr. Kennedy*?"

You. I've been waiting for you my whole life.

Their lips meet in a heated, heavenly kiss that catches in Willow's throat. She whimpers as Chase edges her to the back of the lift, not breaking their kiss, leaving her breathless.

The small sound causes her lips to part, granting him access to her waiting tongue. He knows by the way her body moves in perfect synchronization with his that she, like, has thought about little else than this moment.

The rest of the world fades away. An invisible but irresistible force pulls them together, like gravity. They're back in each other's orbit, slow sensual ellipses of revolution bringing them ever closer until they crash into each other. Chase moves his hands to cup her face, tilting her head ever so slightly to taste as much of her as possible.

His heart beats rapidly as Willow grasps the lapel of his jacket and pulls his body flush with hers. It's been ten years since they'd kissed like this, and Willow's demanding lips are hypnotic and intoxicating.

Kissing Willow Harris isn't like coming home but rather more like exploring the world for the very first time. Her lips hold the answers to man's greatest question, and her tongue holds the secret to the meaning of life.

Kissing Willow Harris is coming up for air after holding his breath underwater. Yes, he's been underwater for a decade, his lungs ready to burst with the pressure. But now he's finally broken through. He can breathe again. He can see the sky after having been submerged for ages in the depths. It's like discovering every color of the rainbow for the very first time. No. More than that. It's like seeing every color ever created, even the ones that the human eye can't detect, all at once. It's euphoric. It's exhilarating. It's transcendent.

It's everything.

Willow Harris is everything.

13

An Owed Explanation

IT'S BEEN SO LONG SINCE Willow's found herself wrapped up in bed with another person. So long that she'd nearly forgotten what it felt like. She smiles to herself and snuggles closer to Chase. There's a not unpleasant flutter of nervousness when he watches her intently.

"What are you thinking about?" Chase asks, the rasp in his deep voice bringing another smile to her lips.

"Nothing."

"Do you always look coy when you think about nothing?" Chase teases.

Willow giggles and tilts her chin up to kiss his cheek. "I'm just recalling a moment very similar to this one, but we were ten—no, eleven—years younger."

"Oh?" He props himself on an elbow and watches her. She looks alluring with her hair spread messily across the sheets beneath her.

"Do you remember how nervous we were back then?" Willow asks with playful mischief in her tone. "The way we fumbled over one another, head over heels and giddy beyond all reason. I still remember how badly my fingers trembled when I tried to undo the buttons on your shirt."

"We were young; we thought we knew *everything* there was to know about love," Chase murmurs. He traces his fingertip along her arm. "But we didn't have any idea what we were doing."

"And now…" Willow's voice trails, allowing the silence to say the unspoken. Now they're grown—lost lovers who found their way back to one another.

In truth, Willow wants to pull him against herself and explore what they'd learned from their time apart, but she doesn't want to rush this moment. So, because she finds it's needed, she reaches forward and kisses him softly against his lips.

"Willow…" he whispers through the kiss.

She pulls back and swallows. "I think we should walk before we run."

Chase nods and pulls her back into the sheets with him. Her throaty laughter rings tenderly against his skin, and he likes that it makes him feel happy and free in this room.

"I've waited ten years; what's one more night?" he teases before pushing himself up from the bed. "Would you like to sleep here tonight, though? You can use an extra toothbrush, and I can lend you a change of clothes."

Willow reaches up for Chase, and he pulls her to her feet. She kisses him again, smiling through it, which makes him chuckle.

"I'll take that as a yes," he mumbles when he pulls away. "C'mon, let me get you that toothbrush."

Willow is the first to wake up in the morning in Chase's arms, where she now realizes she's always belonged. Contentment washes over her as she listens to his steady breathing. *So, this is what it feels like…*

Smiling softly, she drapes her arm across his shoulders and places a slow kiss on the crook of his neck. Chase incoherently mumbles when she does this, and she giggles. "Good morning…"

As she goes for another kiss, he grips her shoulders and pins her down beneath him, trapping her wrist in his hand. His hold is firm but not enough to hurt her, and she is laughing too, and the happiness makes him feel as though his heart is about to burst open.

He smirks more to himself than to her as her eyes grow wide in shock and mischief.

"Just what are you trying to accomplish by kissing me like that, Sweets?"

She wriggles underneath him. "Were my intentions not clear, *Mr. Kennedy?*"

He can see it now; there's a want in her eyes. A desire so wild and vivid it holds him captive. "Willow..." he breathes.

She stops wriggling, and her expression turns serious. *To hell with waiting.* "Kiss me."

Her phone begins to ring, and she rolls her eyes as Chase rolls off her. "You should get that."

"I'd rather not," she says.

"Go ahead, Sweets," he says before gently kissing her shoulder. His finger traces her collarbone, and his voice is a near-whisper when he speaks again. "The sooner the distraction is gone, the sooner we can resume."

Eager to take him up on this, Willow takes her phone from the nightstand and answers it. "Hello?"

"Good morning, Miss Harris! I hope I didn't wake you," the voice is high-pitched and overly excited. "It's Alexandra, Charlotte's wedding planner?" she asks, as though fearing Willow may have forgotten her already.

Willow pushes Chase's wandering hand away from her and sits upright, clutching the sheets. "A-Alexandra?"

Chase also sits upright, his brows furrowed in confusion that mirrors her own.

Alexandra doesn't hesitate in her response. "I know you've already started on some sketches, but Charlotte has just told me she wants to make some changes."

Changes? Uncertainty deepens into feverish fear. Willow glances at Chase when she speaks again, "Charlotte wants to what?"

She watches Chase's face go pale. *Guilt?*

The wedding planner explains that the bride has made new plans. Willow feels herself free falling back to earth.

She can't shake off the feeling of disappointment. The fact that she'd been willing to do anything for Chase stings the most.

A new dress, put on rush order to meet a new date; I must be missing something, right? She searches Chase's gaze, looking for answers but receiving nothing.

Alexandra is still talking. "Would you and your assistant be willing to meet at the couple's residence to make arrangements within the next hour or so?"

Willow swallows. "Um…Yes, I can do that. Send me the address. Lina and I will be there before noon. It's no trouble at all. See you soon, Alexandra."

After she ends the call, she places the phone back down and sighs deeply. Chase's eyes search hers, unsure of what to say, and as question after question floods her mind, she thinks of leaving. Where could she begin anyway?

"That was your wedding planner…" her voice is cold. "Lina and I have to go to your place to discuss a change in plans. Apparently, your wedding has been moved up."

Willow feels a sense of betrayal unlike anything she's ever felt. She steps out of the bed and glares at Chase, crossing her arms over her chest.

Chase, however, is a hundred miles away. Realization fills his eyes as he understands what this means. No one needs to tell him. Charlotte is getting married to the man she'd cheated on him with.

Deafening silence fills the space as Chase folds into himself, body and soul bending into a pained whisper. Truthfully, he'd never thought of Charlotte as someone who'd be capable of doing something like this, especially since it'd been less than twenty-four hours since she'd confessed her infidelities.

She'd called after him in bitter sobs as he'd walked away from her, and today she was planning a wedding with another?

Why does this hurt so much? he asks himself. Even last night, he was so upset when he found out. Yet, he's not blameless either; he's not innocent. He's in love with someone else too.

The only difference is he would never have betrayed Charlotte in this way. He did not betray Charlotte in this way, even though he'd been sorely tempted to do so. Because, despite everything, he'd once loved her too.

Willow's gaze drops, and he sees the sadness in her rigid frame. She doesn't need to say anything; he knows she thinks he's lied to her. Chase edges closer but doesn't touch her. In the end, he has to tell her everything. "Willow, Charlotte had an affair."

Willow's brows crease, but she doesn't say a word. She doesn't want to interrupt his words; she does not want him to leave.

He continues, "Yesterday, I decided to end the engagement. When I explained why we were no longer right for one another, Char—Charlotte—confessed that she'd been having an affair. I ignored the details. It felt like time was standing still. But judging by the moment our relationship started falling out of sync, the affair probably started shortly after our engagement. That's why I came back so late last night. I needed some time to process it."

She can see him as clear as day now. As much as he tries to keep his emotions in check, she can see right through him, knowing his heart is breaking. Hers is also breaking from staring at him and knowing that he still wanted Charlotte in some way and still loved her.

After their reunion in the elevator, the night they spent in one another's arms, and the heated moment they shared this morning, she can see that the news hits him hard.

Did last night mean anything to him? Or had he come into her arms to find a distraction from the warring feelings?

"What does this mean?" she asks if only because merely watching him in silence might kill her. "What does last night mean?"

He frowns hard at her, and for a brief moment, she thinks of saying nothing, but he speaks, and she crashes against herself.

"What do you mean?" he asks.

"Did you..?" she runs a hand through her thick, messy hair. Her confidence dwindles and she suddenly feels sick to her stomach. "I shouldn't have stayed last night."

Chase starts. "What?"

"I should go," she says again.

"Willow," he whispers, and his face changes, and she thinks of his innocent look and his eyes, emitting pain and heartache in so many different ways.

"Willow, please. Don't do this," he says.

"Do what?" she yanks her jeans from the chair and pulls them on. Her voice is rising, but she doesn't seem to care. "Leave before I lose the rest of my dignity?"

She hears him shuffle across the bed behind her, but she's already decided. He walks toward her, closing the distance between them and turns her around before cupping her chin.

"Don't leave me before we can truly begin," he says, and it's a plea. It frightens Chase, and at the moment, he feels cornered because he can feel her slipping away from him a second time. "Please don't walk away from us again."

"Chase..." she licks her lips and looks him dead in the eye.

Perhaps it is selfish, pleading for Willow not to hurt him like she'd hurt him once before, but when he looks at her, he knows he can't lose her.

She swallows. After ten years without each other, she's still afraid to tell him how she truly feels. Ten years of missing him because she'd been too selfish to explain herself. She couldn't do it again. Not to herself and certainly not to Chase.

Taking a deep breath, Willow holds his stare. "Is there even an *us* to walk away from? Are you in the right mind to *actually know* that you want me? How do you know this isn't just seeking comfort in familiar arms? How do you know you won't wake up tomorrow regretting this? How can you know you want *us*?"

"Sweets," he says. "You came back into my life while I was looking for a sign, something to point the way forward in my life. I was going to leave Charlotte regardless of my feelings for you or your feelings for me. Things have been over between us for a long time. If anything, Charlotte's infidelity only confirmed I was right to end the engagement. I didn't leave her because she had an affair, Willow. I left because I hadn't been in love with her for quite some time. I couldn't find a home in her."

He's said the one thing that she's been aching to hear for so long, but Willow doesn't want him to regret this; she doesn't want either of them to regret this. "But how can you know that this is something you want? You say things were over for you two for a long time already—I trust you—but is jumping back to me genuinely something you're sure of?"

He cups her cheeks, his eyes are insistent, and his voice engraves his name on her heart. "Can't you see it, Willow?

Can't you see what you do to me? I never stopped wanting you. I've never stopped loving you."

She longs to lean into his arms and embrace him but holds herself back. "And last night, in the elevator? Was that want, or was that love?"

Chase inclines his head so his lips are an inch away from hers, as he whispers "*Both...Willow...*"

She says nothing, and he pulls back.

"Maybe it was a little rushed, given the day's events," he admits. "But I don't see it as a mistake. For the first time since you walked back into my life, I was finally free to kiss you without guilt. I let my heart take the lead for once. I love you, Willow Harris. Please don't walk out on us."

Love isn't always easy. Willow knows this all too well, but when he looks her in the eye and confesses his love for her, urging her to stay, there's no doubt in her mind that they can't make this work.

"I won't walk out on us," she whispers.

When Chase speaks, he's hesitant. "Do you promise?"

Willow knows that she'll never walk away from him again. Nodding, with no hint of hesitation in her demeanor, she says, "I promise, Chase."

14

Set My Heart Ablaze, Not My Life

"LET ME GET THIS STRAIGHT," Lina starts. She sits cross-legged on the foot of Willow's bed as the designer gets dressed, beaming from ear to ear, and for a moment, Willow pictures Lina holding a giant tub of popcorn in her lap, waiting eagerly for what promises to be a really good show. "Chase and Charlotte are no longer engaged?"

Willow pulls a black turtleneck over her head, shaking the waves that have flattened against her face. "That's right."

Lina leans closer. Willow can practically hear the crunching of the popcorn now. "Charlotte's admitted to having an affair?"

"Yep."

Lina arches an eyebrow and taps her chin. "And we're on our way to discuss a new design for for her to wed her sidepiece in?"

"I mean, is he really a sidepiece if they've been together for a year?" Willow's coy response comes with a matching smile.

Sighing, Lina runs a hand through her hair. The tone of her voice lowers considerably. "You know, when we get there, you should probably avoid smiling so much."

"Is it that obvious?" Willow pouts.

"I mean, we don't know what we're about to walk into, and you're standing there looking like you've just found out your sour aunt died, and you've inherited her millions."

Willow simply shrugs. "I have a plan."

"Oh, do you?" A smile threatens to break out on Lina's red lips. "And what's my part in it?"

"Try your best to hold your sarcastic tongue," Willow teases, despite the anxiousness bubbling in her chest.

When Lina pushes herself off the bed and pulls her into her arms, Willow melts, grateful for her friend's support.

"Welcome, ladies!" Charlotte greets the pair with a breezy wave, welcoming them into her home. "Thank you for coming by on such short notice. I hope we didn't spoil your mornings."

The foyer of the townhouse is large, with a black and white tiled floor and a tall ceiling. There's a winding staircase against the wall with an overwhelming presence, like something out of a Gothic romance novel. A huge bouquet of white peonies sits on the table; a flower choice Willow finds fitting for the blushing bride—the appearance of purity that leaves a sour taste in its wake.

Behind her glasses, Lina squints. She doesn't usually wear these but adds them as a final touch today. "Not at all!"

"We were happy to come in," Willow says brightly. As she does, a tall man strides in confidently, a full smile fills his handsome face. He places a hand on Charlotte's waist, and Willow notices how her cheeks flush at his touch. "Is this the infamous fiancé you've been telling us about?"

Charlotte's smile is proud like she's been waiting for this day all her life, and even though it strangles the happiness inside of Willow, she doesn't show it.

"Ladies, this is Declan Williams."

"Let me take your coats," he says, holding his charming smile in place.

Attentive, Willow thinks. In any case, she's not amused but holds her own tight smile nonetheless. *Just a great big day for smiles, I guess.*

Charlotte chirps busily, "Alexandra is waiting in the dining room."

And in the dining room, Willow observes the new couple closely. As Declan helps Charlotte into her chair and tucks her in before stepping away and settling into his own chair, Willow thinks of Chase and how much he's endured at the hands of this woman.

It breaks her heart yet makes her sure of her feelings for him. He deserves better, and she resolves to give it to him.

The love Charlotte and Declan have for each other is loud and glaring, choking off the air in Willow's lungs. Perhaps their sordid affair wasn't *so* sordid at all. *Still handled it in the shittiest way possible though*, Willow thinks, now actively suppressing the urge to gag.

Still, Willow wants to understand why. Why would Charlotte do this to Chase? Why wouldn't she just break up with him if she was in love with someone else? Surely that would've been easier.

"Well then, shall we get on with the new plan?" Alexandra adjusts her frame in the chair and turns to look at the happy couple as Willow slips into her own chair. "Charlotte, Declan. You expressed wishes for a new date."

Charlotte leans forward, and her expression turns serious. "That's right. We'd like to get married on the sixth of July."

Lina frowns. It's an expression that looks unnatural and out of place compared to the exaggerated smile she usually reserved for clients. "July sixth, as in *three months from now*, July sixth?"

"That's right," Declan says. "Alexandra, I know you originally booked Dartmouth..."

Alexandra cuts him short. "I'm afraid they won't have any availabilities in July. I already had to pull some strings to get the October date."

Declan's smile does not even waver. "That's fine. We're not interested in that venue anymore."

Charlotte helps him. "We want to get married here, in the back garden!"

From across the table, Lina gives Willow the eye. *They are crazy*, she wants to say.

Declan says, "I understand that moving the date up may cause some complications for the dress, but money is no object, Willow. Charlotte expressed how important it is that she wears one of your designs."

"And I've changed my mind on the gown's fit," Charlotte says.

"I see," Willow sighs inwardly. *Of course, she has.* She plasters a smile on her face. "Perhaps you and I can discuss the dress changes privately, Charlotte? Leave it a surprise for Declan?"

"That's a wonderful idea! Come with me!" Charlotte agrees quickly. She rises from her seat and glances at Alexandra and Lina. "Declan will discuss the extra details with you two."

Away from the others in a hall with low lighting, Willow and Charlotte face each other. The corridor is lined with framed photos of Charlotte and Declan, printed in black and white. For a moment, Willow wonders when they were taken, but she quickly clears her throat and looks Charlotte in the eye, focusing on the task at hand.

"Do you think you'll be able to get the dress done in time for the new date?" Charlotte asks, looking up expectantly at her.

Willow shakes her head and looks from side to side as if the very idea of being here with this woman is exhausting. "Charlotte...that is not the man you introduced yesterday. What's going on?"

The bride-to-be doesn't flinch when she responds. "I'm surprised Chase didn't tell you."

It catches Willow off guard. The words are a subtle reminder that nothing is really a secret in the long run, but Willow doesn't want to believe there could be more. "What are you talking about?"

"Do you think I didn't know who you were to him when I hired you?" Charlotte steps away from Willow, her heels leaving a wake of staccato clicks as she walks further down the spacious echoey hall. She pauses and turns to look back at her. "Of course, I knew who you were, Willow. I hired you specifically because of your history with Chase."

Momentarily, Willow stops breathing as her brain processes what she's heard. It's like a scene from an old movie or a soap opera. The more she thinks about the past couple of days, and the events leading up to it, the more monstrous Charlotte's lie becomes. How could she have known? And what sort of psycho puts into action a scheme so complex and hurtful, so *cruel*, just to spare themselves a painful breakup? Was this her version of being *nice*? *What's she like when she's mean?* Willow thinks and immediately has to suppress a shudder.

Charlotte senses her mood and sees her steadily darkening countenance but forges ahead regardless. "He told me about you when we first started dating. Right after I opened up to him about Declan."

"I don't understand," says Willow warily. She takes a hesitant step forward, careful as though she's walking into a trap. *Another* trap.

"We're not that different, you and I," Charlotte says softly. "I left the love of my life to pursue an education in Chicago. And in doing so, I met Chase. I fell in love with him. But I knew from the moment he told me about you that he would never fully belong to me. And yet, I still tried. I really did. I held on to the dream of us. When he proposed to me last year, I thought he was finally ready to let go of you"—she smiles sadly—"But it turned out that *I* wasn't ready to let go. I returned to London, and Declan returned to me. I knew my relationship with Chase was over the moment I saw Delcan."

Willow hasn't been defensive with her before, but Charlotte's words make her heartbeat spike, awash in confusion and anger as her mind focuses on Chase and the pain held in his eyes while his tormentor is right here in front of her. She swallows up her pride. Everything is out now, so she reckons there's no need to pretend anymore.

"Why didn't you end your relationship with Chase?" she asks, aware that her voice is up an octave, but not really caring. Nor does Charlotte, if her cool exterior is anything to go by. *Butter wouldn't melt in this bitch's mouth.* "Why string him along for the past year?"

"You didn't see what you did to him!" Charlotte snaps. "I'm *not* a bad person, Willow. I'll admit," she says, shrugging with an air of glib concession, "I *may* have gone about this in the wrong way. But do you really think he would have survived another heartbreak? I knew if you walked back into his life, he would be okay. Because while Chase loved me, he was never *in* love with me, you see? Do you understand?"

Willow says nothing because no matter how hard she tries, the words won't come.

"He went to you last night, didn't he?" Charlotte asks.

"He did," Willow affirms, her tone quiet and neutral.

Uncertain how to interpret this response, Charlotte asks, "Do you still love him?"

"Yes," she responds without hesitation. "I always will."

A small smile lifts the corners of Charlotte's mouth, and she sighs happily. It is a very smug sound, the contentedly triumphant purr of the cat who ate the canary and got away with it. "Good," Charlotte breathes out, noticeably relaxing. Then, so quickly and sharply that it almost makes Willow jump, Charlotte claps her hands together, her face fixed in a kind of gleeful rictus. "Now then, shall we discuss the dress?"

Willow arches an eyebrow, surprised the deal is still on after everything. It feels ethereal having discussed something as profound as this with her client, but it also makes her happy in an admittedly surreal way. "You still want a dress from me?"

"Of course I do. While I hired you to bring you back into his life, I still adore your designs."

"The deadline…" Willow's voice trails before she says what she's really thinking—*not to mention the colossal conflict of interest.*

Charlotte's hands instinctively come around to her flat stomach and a broader smile forms, changing her face completely—she looks younger. Willow can see why Chase was smitten with her.

"I know it's a tight deadline," Charlotte continues, "but we must marry soon. We're expecting a little one come autumn."

"A little one—" Willow's eyes widen as she watches Charlotte's hand gently stroke her stomach. "You're pregnant?! Is—does Chase know?"

Charlotte waves her hand dismissively. "It doesn't concern him."

Willow wants to say so much more, but the answer, the words, everything comes all at once. "It doesn't—What? You two don't...? Is there a possibility that Chase is the father?"

"Chase doesn't need to know this, Willow," Charlotte's tone is low, leaving little room for argument. Unfortunately for her, Willow doesn't care. She's done caring. She's done nothing but care for the past two days, and she has no more fucks to give, certainly, at least, where Charlotte is concerned.

"How can you say that?"

"Declan and I are raising this baby together, regardless of paternity."

"Chase deserves to know if it's his!"

Charlotte's smile is gone now, replaced by a murderous glare. "This doesn't concern *you!*"

Willow laughs coldly. She's not about to back down, especially not where Chase is concerned, especially not for this *thing* in front of her. A wave of revulsion washes over Willow, and when the wave breaks, the world is different. The woman standing in front of her isn't beautiful, and Willow finds herself wondering how and why she ever thought she was. "You made this my concern the moment you disclosed this to me!"

Charlotte swallows, and her gaze lowers to the floor. "The only thing that you need to be concerned with is making sure I have a dress made in time for the wedding."

"A dress?" Willow scoffs, and her expression changes swiftly to one of repulsion. She'd considered Charlotte a good person—before this morning. She was willing to give her the benefit of the doubt. But hearing this changes everything. "If you think I'm going to design your wedding dress after dragging me into this mess, you are mistaken."

"Very well then," Charlotte nods curtly. "Consider our contract null." She steps closer to Willow, lowering her voice and narrowing her eyes. "But you'd better not breathe a word of what you've learned today to Chase," she hisses conspiratorially.

Willow holds the stare, her heartbeat now steady with the cold fury of righteous indignation. *You hurt Chase. You're hurting him still, and you either don't see it or don't care.* "Oh no, honey. You don't get to intimidate me. If you don't tell Chase you might be carrying his child, I will."

15

Complications of a Healthy Relationship

Twelve years ago...

"IS THAT *UNDER THE MOON?*"

Willow glanced up past the pages of the book she'd been lost in. She was met with an intense gaze framed by long eyelashes. Her eyes searched the empty aisle around them at the back of the bookstore that her new, elderly neighbor suggested she check out.

"Well?" the boy asked. There was a hint of a smile playing at the corner of his mouth.

"It is," Willow responded. She blinked, lowering the book to get a better look at the interloper.

"Mind if I take a quick look?"

"You want to take a look at this exact copy?" she asked, making a point to look at the several other copies just to the left of her.

He shrugs. "It's life or death, really. You have a chance to save a life."

"Is that so?"

"Yeah, you wouldn't want to be responsible for my death, would you?"

Willow fought back a smile. Taking a mental note to remember the page number she was on—thirty-two—she turned the book over to the strange boy. "Murderer isn't exactly how I plan to be remembered, so here."

The boy smirked, taking the book from her hands. His fingers brushed against hers, and Willow held her breath, which he noticed.

"And how is it that you want to be remembered?" he asked, flipping through the pages. "Cause I can tell you right now, I know how I'll be remembering you."

"How's that?"

Pulling a pen from his pocket, the boy begins to write on the book's inside cover.

"What are you—"

"I'll remember you as the most beautiful woman I've ever seen," he said, smiling as he closed the book and placed it back in Willow's grasp.

"That's so cheesy," Willow retorted.

"Well, judging from the pink on your cheeks, I think you're probably a fan of cheese."

Then, smiling broadly, the boy turned on his heel and walked away. Willow blinked, torn between genuine curiosity about him and a little concern about the place her parents have moved their family to.

But when she opened the book to see the note, her stomach flipped, and she thought that perhaps Portland wouldn't be so bad.

"I was trying to read you," Chase says, laughing at the story. He'd been the one to initiate the FaceTime call this morning, eager to see her again. "God, the way you kept up with me, too. I knew I had to know you."

Sitting alone in her room with the phone in front of her, Willow shakes her head, "You took the book and wrote your number in it!"

"Yeah, that was a bit cringe, wasn't it?" he laughs.

A small smile forms on her lips. "Well, you did get my number in the end."

"Sweets," he says, leaning forward. "I'm embarrassed for you! You're the one who said yes to the lamest pickup ever!"

"And look at us now!"

"And look at us now."

How far they've come. Now, years later, when Willow replays the memory in her head, she finds that she's more than grateful for the meet and the love that grew from it, making her the happiest she's ever been.

"I want to see you tonight," Chase says after a while.

"Alright, how about dinner?" Willow asks, then—deciding to dive in head first—adds, "My place?"

He shakes his head, an idea already forming at the back of his mind. "Actually, I was wondering if you'd like to come to mine. I'd like to make you dinner."

She clasps her wrist and laughs excitedly. "I won't say no to that. I'll bring dessert."

A small smile tugs at the corners of his lips. You are the dessert, he wants to say, but instead, he says, "No need, Sweets. I've got that covered too. During my first year here, I found this little bakery with the best dairy-free ganache in the world."

"Alright then, it's a date!"

Work is the one thing that gets Willow to calm down, the only thing that'll distract her from her warring thoughts. As she walks into her boutique, located in the heart of Chicago's Magnificent Mile, she feels a peace wash over her.

She's worked hard to create her ideal space, a critical part of her ideal life. Willow smiles as she recalls the late nights spent with Lina, painting the walls in bright pinks, oranges, and purples. Each client that comes in is greeted by the shades of a perfect sunset. It's fun, just like their experience with Willow and Lina should be, and almost invariably is.

"Morning, Wills!" Lina's cheery greeting rings through the display room.

"Hello, hello," Willow nods cheerfully. "How's it going?"

As if on cue, Lina yawns. "I could use a nap."

"Already?" she laughs.

"You look like you could, too. Did you get any sleep last night?" The concern in Lina's voice is evident, but Willow waves her off, not wanting to dive into it right now.

"What's on the agenda today? Maybe we can sneak out early." The suggestion has a selfish notion behind it, but Lina's smile is reassuringly conspiratorial.

"Only Opal's final fitting, which is at two. I took a peek at your inbox, and you're starting to get a pretty sizable influx of queries, spring engagements and whatnot, so I figured it's best to keep the schedule light."

"I don't know what I did to deserve you, but it was worth it." Willow smiles, pushing her hair back and tying it into a messy bun. "I'd better dive in, then."

Willow makes a beeline for the solace of her studio. She doesn't want to explain the exhaustion written on her face, though she's sure Lina already suspects the reason.

She has avoided speaking about the situation with Chase and Charlotte since they left Charlotte's home. But it's kept her up at night, tossing and turning for the past week since she returned to Chicago.

Getting Chase off her mind is nearly impossible, and Willow misses him a lot more than she thought she would. If she's not longing to lose herself in his embrace again, her mind reels under the heavy burden of the secret pregnancy Charlotte imposed on her.

A secret pregnancy that Charlotte couldn't even confirm the paternity of. Chase could—

Willow shakes her head. "Nope. Do not even *think* about going there."

"Are you talking to the mannequins again?" Willow turns to see Lina leaning against the doorframe, arms crossed, a perfectly threaded eyebrow raised. "You really need to start letting other human beings in here, Wills." She steps into the studio and places her hands on the table. "What's on your mind?"

Willow rubs the back of her neck and holds her breath for a moment. There's no obvious meaning behind why she does this, but it helps her, in some way, to stay afloat and not sink in the pain and uncertainty of what may lie ahead. "Chase invited me over for dinner today."

"Wow, he's not playing around, huh?" Lina flashes a wicked grin, letting Willow know exactly where her mind's just gone.

Willow shakes her head and shuffles her feet against the floor. "I just...I don't know if Charlotte has talked to him about..."

And her voice trails off. She can't bear to say it out loud.

But Lina, apparently, can. "Is it the whole possible baby-daddy mess?"

Willow shrugs, but the answer is on her lips before she can wave it off. "It's all I can think about."

"Then tell him."

Lina has never been one to shy away from confronting a problem head-on or avoid dealing with a hard truth, and most often, Willow follows her advice. It's not as simple this time around, though. The last thing she wants to do is hurt Chase, and she knows this will break him.

Sensing Willow's indecision, Lina tries to put her point across. "You told Charlotte that if she didn't tell Chase, you would. It's been a week; she hasn't told him."

Willow instinctively runs a hand through her hair and sighs wearily. "Isn't that cruel? I mean, is it really my news to tell?"

Lina shakes her head and draws closer. "What's cruel is hiding a baby from its father. Think of it from his perspective. You knew his ex-fiancée was pregnant, but you chose to ignore it to enjoy your bliss bubble for as long as possible."

As plausible as this argument sounds, Willow is not so sure about it. "That's not true."

"No, but that's how he'll read it if you don't follow through and tell him. Or, you could tell him tonight, and avoid a *really* unnecessary conflict." Lina gently presses a hand against her shoulders, and her expression softens considerably. "Willow, Chase loves you. If Charlotte won't tell him, then it's up to you."

Willow groans. She knows Lina's right. But rarely is the right thing easy, and this certainly won't be. *Why can't the right thing and the thing I want to do ever be the same thing?*

"What if I tell him and he leaves me?" she asks and—before Lina can interject—adds, "I know how selfish that sounds, trust me. I feel sick just thinking about it, let alone vocalizing it. But I'm—I'm scared, Lina. I feel like I just got him back."

Lina blows out a breath, letting Willow's fears settle into the space around them. "I don't know, Wills. But you won't go through it alone, okay? I promise."

Her statement brings Willow a bit of comfort, and she offers her friend a small smile in return, nodding. "Okay."

"Personally? I don't think he'll leave you. Because, one, I don't think you two reuniting after all this time makes sense, especially in how it happened, if it wasn't fate. And two, have you seen the way that man looks at you? Because I have. He's smitten, Willow. He's not going *anywhere*."

"Alright, alright," Willow rolls her eyes at Lina's teasing, fighting the blush threatening to bloom on her. "I guess you have a point."

Lina shrugs off the concession with good-natured dismissal. "I have my moments. You both agreed to give your relationship a fresh start, right? Well, a good relationship is built on a foundation of trust and communication," Lina states. "Just tell him how you're feeling."

"Isn't it a little early for pre-marriage counseling?" Willow asks, scrunching her nose.

Lina laughs heartily, shaking her head no. "This relationship has been on hold for ten years, Wills. It's not too early for anything."

16

Let's Lose Ourselves Tonight

WILLOW HOLDS A GIFT BAG containing the bottle of white wine she's decided to bring along for dinner. Chase may have insisted he take care of everything, but her mother always taught her not to show up empty-handed when invited to someone's home.

As she knocks on the large walnut door to Chase's condo, she distracts herself from her nerves by glancing around the vast corridor. There are only three other condos on this floor, and based on the presence of the doorman in front of the luxurious building, Willow assumes that the people who reside here come from wealth. The idea that Chase has done well enough for himself to afford this building fills her with pride.

She lets herself imagine, just for a moment, what it would be like to call this place home. Would they spend their evenings cuddling on the couch, watching TV, or dancing in the kitchen? Would Sunday afternoons be their designated grocery trip to the supermarket a block away? Would they host her dad and siblings for the holidays? Though comforted by this fantasy, she knows she can't hide from reality.

Because the reality is Willow will not see this fantasy come true if she doesn't go through with the decision to tell Chase about Charlotte's pregnancy. How can she dream of a shared future when his own future is still so uncertain? Selfishly, Willow wants him all to herself. But the genuine possibility of Chase being a father looms over her, and she knows they can't have a future until he knows the truth.

Heavy footsteps approaching the other side of the door tell Willow that Chase is near. She rolls her shoulders back and smiles softly, excited to see the face she's been missing so badly.

When he finally opens the door, his smile widens, and she thinks of sinking into his arms but stops herself midway and holds up the gift bag. "I brought wine."

"Hello to you too, Sweets," Chase laughs, holding his smile in place. He steps aside, welcoming her into his home. "May I take your coat?"

Just beyond the threshold, there are several boxes stacked in the corner. Willow's brows arch. "Did you recently move in?"

"No, that's just Charlotte's stuff. I'm shipping it to her tomorrow," he says dismissively, as though it doesn't matter that he's packed up five years of his life with someone else. With Willow's coat hung, he turns to her. "Come on," he says, nodding his head toward the hall, "I hope you're hungry."

He leads her down the hall and into the open space of his living area. Willow pauses, taking it all in. With dark-stained hardwood floors paired with dark furniture and black marble accents, the condo feels more like a bachelor's home than that of a couple; well-placed lighting and huge windows lining the west wall save the condo from the total darkness threatening to overtake the…*man cave? Yeah. Very tastefully appointed, but yeah. Definitely the house of a single man.*

When she steps into the grand kitchen, she's met with the sight of Chase tying an apron around his waist. The kitchen, she knows, is one of the most intimate places in a house, and his invitation here means so much more to her than dinner at a restaurant.

"Chase, this place is huge!" she gasps. "How long have you lived here?"

"I moved in right before Thanksgiving last year," he answers, turning around the kitchen like it's his first time here as well. There's pride in his voice. "It was my first big purchase after I made partner—the youngest at the firm, I might add."

She crosses her arms and tries to hide her smile, but she feels pride for his growth, for how he's been able to move away from so many problems and become this version of a man. "That's pretty impressive, Mr. Kennedy."

"Willow..." he begins but stops when she moves away to pour the wine into the glasses he's set out. She passes one to him and holds one close to her.

"You know what's more impressive?" Her smile is wide like she's going to burst into resounding laughter any minute, and even though he does not know why, he smiles back, too excited to think about anything else.

"What's that?" he asks.

She eases closer, and her eyelids droop. "You in an apron."

Chase pulls back quickly and looks down at his frame, laughing at his forgetfulness. He does a little spin for her, much to her delight. "Drink your wine, crazy girl. I'm just finishing up here."

Willow clinks her glass against his. "What's on the menu tonight?"

"I'm making a stir fry bowl," he replies. "How was work today?"

"Can I sit here?" she asks, pointing to a stool by the island.

"Make yourself at home, Sweets," he says a little forcefully, and she laughs before settling down on the stool. He smiles lazily, watching her. "I like seeing you sit there."

His gentle confession catches Willow off guard. "Do you?"

"It's a dream come true," he answers immediately.

Willow blushes. It feels so surreal to be here with Chase like this. Giddy, she moves the glass of wine to the side and leans out of her chair, resting her palms on the cool countertop. "I'd very much like to kiss the chef now, please."

She sees him swallow before a cocky smirk crosses his face. "The chef is happy to oblige."

An hour passes by in a blink, and both of them catch up on their week apart. After dinner, Chase leads Willow to the living room. They settle down on one of the couches and she nestles closer as he wraps his arm around her.

Chase absentmindedly plays with Willow's hair. The moment is so simple and intimate Willow's heart swells with joy. It feels like this is the way things were always supposed to be. When she glances up at Chase, she's met with a soft smile.

"What are you thinking about right now?" she asks.

"Would it be completely cheesy to tell you how glad I am that you're here?" He wrestles with the idea for a moment and whispers it out to her. "Next to me, in my home. It's like life is finally falling into place."

Her smile drops, and she shifts away from him. The weight of Charlotte's secret comes back tenfold, and Willow wallows in her guilt. She's put the conversation off for as long as she can, possibly longer than she should have. "Chase, I..." she sighs and starts again. "Have you heard from Charlotte this week?"

"No," he shrugs. "I doubt she'll try to contact me. I told her I never wanted to hear from her again." He looks at her quizzically, confused at the introduction of a topic in which he very specifically has no interest. "Why do you ask?"

The last thing she wants to do is hurt him, but she must tell the truth. "I need to tell you something, and I'm not really sure how."

Chase sits upright and stretches out to take her hands in his. He squeezes gently and looks deep into her eyes.

"I want you to feel comfortable telling me anything, Willow." His voice is soft and comforting. It makes her stomach twist. She swallows the lump that's formed in her suddenly dry throat.

Pulling her hands away from his, she sits up straight. *There's no going back now.*

"As you know, I went to Charlotte's home to discuss some changes to her wedding dress..." she begins. "You were right. She's marrying the other man."

He swallows but says nothing, which is her cue to continue.

"When we walked in, she introduced us to the man as if it was the most normal thing in the world. As if she hadn't introduced Lina and me to you the morning prior."

"That's not surprising," he whispers. "She's always been a master at saving face." There's the slightest hint of pride in his voice, as though he recalls a moment the skill was of use to him.

Willow can feel the truth and pain bubbling deep inside, threatening to fall, but there is no stopping now. "Well, it gets more complicated," she continues. "The reason she's decided to change the dress is because she's moving up the wedding date. And...the reason she's moving it up is because...she's pregnant."

When his smile wavers, Willow holds her breath, waiting for the shock to settle in. She can only imagine what's going on inside his mind. He watches her, his eyes moving frantically around her face as though he's trying to grasp the reality of her words. When his face pales, she grabs his hand and presses a tentative kiss to his palm as though it can stop the pain and anger.

"Chase?" she whispers.

He gets up from the couch and shakes his head. "I'm calling her."

"I'll excuse myself," she whispers and rises to leave, but he stops her, his arms clinging to her body in desperation.

"No, please," Chase mutters under his breath. "Please stay."

"I'll stay," she whispers. It's the only thing he has to tell her. "I'm going to top off our wine; I have a feeling we'll need it."

After Willow brushes past him and into the kitchen, Chase calls Charlotte. She finally answers on the fourth ring.

"It's Chase," he says.

"Chase?" She sounds uncertain. "It's two in the morning. Is everything okay?"

"I don't know, Charlotte. Why don't you tell me? Have you been feeling alright? Nauseous, perhaps?"

"Willow told you," she states matter-of-factly. He finds that she isn't surprised in the least.

"She shouldn't have had to," he says bitterly. He wants to scream at her, but Chase keeps his emotions in check because of Willow.

"I'm sorry, Dar—Chase," her voice breaks in half.

Once, not that long ago, the break in her voice would have tugged at his heartstrings, but now, it only annoys him. "Whose is it?"

She releases a small sigh of defeat—a sigh which, in a way, confirms his assumptions. But Chase wants answers. It's a need surpassing every other thought, and so he waits, pressing the phone hard against his ear.

Finally, a soft reply meets his ear, "I—I don't know."

It's not the answer he expected. The fear seeps in now, and he loses himself, screaming, "You don't know?! How—how far along are you? When—?"

She doesn't hesitate. "Christmas."

Shit. In a last-minute decision, he had flown out to spend the holiday with Charlotte and her parents. Things between them were heading downhill, so he'd thought a grand gesture would help reignite the spark. It had, but apparently a little too well.

"Look, I know this isn't what you expected. But even if it is yours, you're off the hook."

A frown creases his brows, but he keeps his voice level. "*Excuse me?*"

She says, "The baby. We'll raise them, and you don't even have to contribute financially."

He swallows. "*We*, as in you and your boyfriend?"

"My fiancé, yes."

"If you think I'm not going to be involved with my child, you're delusional."

"Chase, come on," she almost sounds tired, sad even. "You don't want a child."

Chase is shaking from the words bubbling inside of his throat. "I thought you knew me better than this, Char. Regardless of what I've said in the past, I would never abandon a child."

"Please don't make this more complicated than it needs to be," she pleads softly, and he hears a ruffle in the background. There's someone else with her.

"You made this more complicated the moment you tried to hide a fucking *pregnancy* from me!" he snaps.

It takes a while before she speaks again; when she does, it's a whisper. "It's late, and I need to get back to sleep, Chase."

"I want a paternity test," he blurts out thoughtlessly.

"You'll have to wait. It's harmful to the baby during pregnancy," she retorts.

Frustrated, he sighs. "When are you due?"

"Early September."

"Fine," he says, tired himself now and a little defeated. "I'll let you go. But Charlotte?"

"Yes?"

"We will be discussing this," he says through gritted teeth before dropping the call.

He stares blankly at the floor, repeatedly replaying the conversation, knowing he could become a father in five short months. Never one to envision a white-picket-fence future, the last thing Chase thought he would do was start a family, but with the end of the call comes the harrowing thought that the chances of fatherhood are fifty-fifty for him.

I can't be a father, he thinks. *I just got Willow back.*

"This isn't how it was supposed to go," he groans.

"Chase?" Willow calls. She approaches him cautiously as he turns to face her.

He's exhausted, of course, but the anger is real and intense. "Charlotte doesn't know who the father is."

"It's okay," she tries again.

He shakes his head. "No, it's not. How could she just hide that from me? What kind of a person does that? I can't believe she doesn't know whose it is," he says bitterly. "I can't believe she was unfaithful!"

"Chase, stop," Willow whispers. "Take a breath."

"This wasn't the way things were supposed to happen!"

She says nothing. What is there to say in a moment like this, anyway?

"I finally got you back, Willow!" he says, and it feels as though he's screaming, but he's laughing and crying at the same time. "I finally got you back."

Wordlessly, Willow steps closer to Chase and lays her hands against his chest. He meets her gaze; his dark like the ocean at midnight, filled with anger, betrayal, and defeat. Hers an early dawn filled with concern, heartache, and empathy but also comfort, hope, and possibility.

Taking a deep breath, she wraps a hand around his neck and pulls him closer to her. She kisses his cheek slowly, willing him to hear her through her actions. Her lips trace his jawline as she toys with the hair at the nape of his neck.

She pulls back, her lips a fraction away from his. His unsteady breath mingles with hers as they stare silently at each other. Chase finds it hard to articulate his needs proper words, to conjure up the magic words that will make this moment okay.

"You still have me, Chase," Willow whispers, and even though it's an effort to comfort him and to show him she'll stay regardless, it's also a promise to keep him safe and close.

Chase doesn't wait anymore. His lips find hers, and he presses her closer, moving together in perfect synchronization.

An all too familiar surge courses through their bodies as the kiss deepens and instinct takes control. Chase tugs her hair gently, tentatively, exposing her neck to him while his tongue trails a line along her jaw.

Her fingers toy with the hem of his shirt until she gives up and tries to bunch it up above his head. With a nod of encouragement, he sweeps her into his arms and carries her to the other side of his home.

Everything about Willow only heightens his mood, further honing the edge of already razor-sharp desire. Barely three steps into the bedroom, Chase has her pressed against the wall. His eyes take her in, drinking in her trembling lips, widened gaze, and ruffled hair. He can't get enough of her; he only wants to forget the world around him and get lost in her.

And then his lips hastily meet hers, and the moment they do, it feels like the world falls away.

His tongue slips between her lips, exploring her mouth with an urgent hunger. Willow grips his shoulders to bring his body flush against hers. The kiss is a plea to be saved, touched, and wanted intimately; somehow, it feels as though it's everything they've been waiting for all their lives. Perhaps, in a sense, they have. Each minute that passes washes away the memory of any other kiss they've shared with others, cleansing them so that they may truly begin again. All that exists tonight is their love.

When he breaks the kiss, they're both breathless. "I love you, Willow Harris," he says, and he means it. He'll forget everything else tonight and reintroduce himself to her, connecting on the deepest level of two souls and bodies becoming one. Her eyes tell him she wants that too, and it fills him with an emotion so complex and profound, he isn't even sure there's a word for it.

"I love you, Chase Kennedy."

17

There's No Coming Back From This

CHASE DREAMS ABOUT WILLOW leaving him. It's different from the typical nightmare he used to have where the failed proposal would haunt him. This time, the present makes an appearance. She walks back into his life, and they're happy. But it doesn't last. She leaves him again, only this time, it's because of *him*.

"I don't want this," she says. *"I don't want you."*

No matter what he says, no matter what he does, Willow always leaves.

"I don't want you."

He wakes up with a groan. Beads of sweat break against his forehead, but when he turns on his side, Willow's there, her hair plastered on the pillow and sheets. It takes a second for his brain to register this, but his heartbeat steadies when he does.

Slowly Chase eases out of the silk sheets, careful not to wake her as he enters the ensuite.

Under the solace of hot water, he wonders why the memory hasn't yet faded and why his subconscious would remind him of Willow's rejection. Perhaps, he reckons, it's the result of the news or the change he can feel on the horizon.

The change. The baby. The child that might be mine. Chase closes his eyes and tilts his face up toward the stream of water. *This is fear of the unknown. Willow's with me; she's happy, she's not going anywhere.*

"Need a hand?" Willow's dreamy voice meets him in the shower. He wonders if he's conjured her. Then she swipes the soapy loofah across his shoulders, and he smirks.

Turning, he pulls her into his arms before losing himself in her welcome kiss. Ultimately, she's become the only person who can cleanse his mind from the lingering effects of the nightmare. With her close to his chest, he tries to remind himself she isn't the same girl who left him a decade ago and prays she won't prove him wrong.

At work, Chase attempts to bury himself in his case files to avoid the mess of his personal life. He wants to be able to breathe easy, even for just a little while.

His legal secretary, Arina, pops her head in through the half-open door, and he waves her in.

"You have a lunch meeting with Carter tomorrow, contract negotiation," she says. She has her hair in a ponytail, professional looking in every aspect, but somehow his mind keeps going back to Willow. He wants to know everything about her and rid himself of the fear that she might leave again, and Chase lets this preoccupation swallow him whole.

Arina is still talking. "And then you need—Chase." She pauses, arching an eyebrow. "I love being ignored when I'm talking. It's just the best." Then, when he still doesn't respond, "Earth to Chase Kennedy!"

He shakes his head and leans back against his seat. "Oh sorry, Arina. Can we do this later? I need some space."

She sighs, resisting the urge to roll her eyes, only partially succeeding. "Don't forget you have an eleven o'clock in the conference room."

"Right, thanks."

Chase welcomes the enveloping silence that falls so neatly across his office, like a comforting blanket. His weekend with Willow, wonderful as it was, has done nothing to ease the whispers of uncertainty chattering incessantly in the darker recesses of his mind, and as he checks his phone for what seems to be the hundredth time that morning, he feels his mood plummet even further into despair. He's left Charlotte a dozen voicemails and countless texts, all of which remain unanswered.

But he's not the only one being left unread. The text Willow sent him this morning is still untouched in his inbox. It isn't because he doesn't want to respond to her; he does. But he doesn't know what to say, not when he can't stop thinking about the baby and the possibility that his life might turn upside down in a few months. How can he drag her into this mess? How can she possibly be okay with it?

Placing his phone face down in front of him, Chase relaxes against his seat. Involuntarily, his mind begins replaying the events that had somehow led him here to this point, a kind of horrible home video that he doesn't remember producing and certainly didn't ask for, one of those things that makes him wonder if his own mind actually hates him because that is the only explanation for this memory loop of misery that makes any kind of sense to him. It seems to him that the universe is testing his patience, and at this moment, he realizes he's never felt so lost.

Obviously, the movie starts years back, ten to be precise, when he first decided to move away following Willow's rejection. His parents hadn't been keen on the idea.

"Must you really go through with this, Chase?" his mother had asked him, exhausted from the bickering.

His father nudged her softly. "Sandra, we agreed to be supportive."

She rolled her eyes, and Chase felt a pang of guilt for having put them in this position. "He's moving to Chicago, Garth. To become a damn lawyer! I thought this nonsense would be over and done with by now."

"Why don't you tell me how you really feel, Mom?" Chase quipped, perhaps a bit too snarkily. But he'd been eating this kind of talk for weeks now without saying a word, and he was finally full.

His father's eyes flashed, and he sidled forward between Chase and his mother. "You would do well to watch your tone, young man."

"I can look past the switching states, really," his mother interjected. "But I don't understand why you would change your career plan. I thought you wanted to go into medicine?"

Chase ran a shaky hand through his hair and blew the air out of his lungs. Looking back at his parents, he felt trapped, like an animal searching for shelter and not finding it, but he'd decided long ago not to back down.

He said, "Don't you think it's weird that you're more focused on my career choice than you are on my moving out of state? You raised an independent person, yet you're complaining because I've chosen my own path?"

"Chase, enough." His father's tone was raised but not so much as to become unrecognizable. "Your mother and I are just worried you're switching majors impulsively."

"Every decision you've been making for the past three years has been impulsive," his mother finally snapped.

"Excuse me?" The words caught in his throat, and for the very first time, Chase wanted to scream at her.

She continued, her voice ragged with the exhaustion of frustrated maternal worry. "We don't know who you are anymore, Chase. You can't keep pining after her."

He crossed his arms, edging closer. "You can say her name, Mom. I won't break."

"That's enough, Chase!" His father said, properly angry now. "I will not tolerate your attitude any longer! We get it. Willow broke your heart. But at some point, you need to move on with your life. You're twenty-one years old, for God's sake. You have your whole life ahead of you. Your life did not end just because your first love left you."

Chase had mapped out his entire life with Willow, and she'd ended it, and everything afterward had led him to this point in every way.

Since the day he left Portland, Chase's relationship with his parents has been less than ideal. In fact, it's Charlotte who helped mend his relationship with them. The moment he brought her home, they treated her like a member of the family. She fit in so well with his little tribe; it was one of the things Chase loved about her.

That may change now. Though he's yet to inform his parents of the recent change of events, Chase can't bring himself to make the call. He knows they'll ask why he hasn't fought for Charlotte, why he's choosing to go back to the woman who previously ripped his heart to shreds. Truthfully, he doesn't know what to say to them.

Even the knowledge of Charlotte's infidelity likely won't change how his parents feel about her, especially with the possibility of a grandchild thrown into the mix. He can hear his mother saying, "Oh, Chase, honey, we all make mistakes. Relationships take work. You shouldn't give up at the first sign of trouble." And yet, Chase was dead certain, she wouldn't stand behind that statement if it was about Willow.

Deep in thought, Chase doesn't hear the rapping on his door until it opens, and he sees the face of his friend, Beck.

"How did I know you would be holed up in here?" Beck teases, sitting on the chair opposite him.

Chase smiles, too, briefly. "How did I know you would walk in here without knocking?"

"I knocked," he says defensively, laughing. "And what kind of friend would I be if I didn't check in on you?" Beck crosses his arms; his expression turns serious. "I don't think I have to tell you you've been weird all week."

Groaning, Chase asks, "How bad is it?"

"Bad enough that Daphne almost came in here instead of me."

Chase flinches. The idea of his managing partner walking in to scold him makes his skin crawl.

"Luckily, I convinced her not to," Beck continues. "But you need to get it together, man. What's going on with you?

You're walking around like you have a huge chip on your shoulder. The last time you acted this way was when you were running away from...."

His voice trails off, and Chase knows he'll not continue even if there's more he wants to say. Chase met his mentor shortly after he arrived in Chicago, back when he was a shell of a man looking for meaning in all the wrong places. Beck had seen a part of himself in the young man; he, too, had once been lost. Perhaps that's what drew him to take Chase under his wing.

Chase had spent his days as a dutiful student in preparation for his career, but his nights were a different story. They were nights spent in search of distraction. In a sense, Chase had fled Portland to flee his memories of Willow, looking to fill the void with anyone else, to forget her altogether. But he'd tasted her in the kiss of every stranger, embracing the tricks his mind played on him.

"Did something happen between you and Willow?" Beck's question drags Chase out of his thoughts again. "I told you to tread carefully with her, Chase. I swear if she ran off on you again..."

He had, too. The moment Chase told Beck about Willow's reappearance, Beck had warned him. His mind wracked with second thoughts, Chase wonders if he should've listened.

"Char is pregnant," he finally says.

Beck blinks. "Oh, uh, congratulations?"

"She doesn't know who the father is."

"Well, this explains everything."

Chase sighs. "She's been ignoring all my calls and messages. I don't know what to do."

Beck leans forward and places his hands against the table. "Well, first things first, you need to get your head right. You've been pulled through the wringer and you need to reprioritize."

"How do I know what needs to be a priority?"

"That's really up to you," Beck says. "My only advice is to follow your intuition. What has your gut been telling you?"

Chase's phone chimes, and he groans.

"Charlotte?" Beck asks.

"Willow. We're having dinner tonight," he says, running a hand over his face.

Beck sees the torn look of desperation etched on his face. He wants to say more but allows Chase to make his own decision. All Beck can do now is keep his phone on for Chase.

The invitation to dinner at Willow's should've made Chase giddy, but as he rings the doorbell, the only thing he can think about is Charlotte continuing to leave him in the dark.

Willow wraps her arms around him when she opens the door, and he kisses her cheeks. Inside her home, she says, "I thought we could have a drink before we head out. I don't know about you, but I could use one after the day I had at work. Whoever said working with brides would be a step in the right direction has clearly never worked with brides before."

He isn't listening; she can see it. She swallows and draws closer. "Chase?"

He looks up at her. "Hmm? Yes?"

"Would you like a drink?"

"Uh yeah, sure. A drink sounds good. You happen to have any scotch?"

"Shelf above you," she says.

She takes him to the kitchen as he'd done when she first went to his place, and when she leans against the kitchen cabinet, he smiles, and it seems like he means it. "You have quite the home, Willow."

"Thank you!" she smiles, beaming proudly. She loves her home, and she loves sharing it with him. From the large, healthy houseplants such as the Monstera growing in the corner and the velvety calathea vines that sit over the custom limewashed cabinets, it's clear she's put in a lot of work to make this space her own.

"You even have a good-sized yard," he muses, nodding toward the large patio doors leading into a cozy, manicured backyard.

"A little peace and quiet for those hectic days. We can sit out on the deck if you'd like," Willow suggests, passing him the drink. "Here, make yourself at home."

"Thanks," he says and moves out of the kitchen. Chase slips out through the patio door by the side of the house and moves to the back, stealing a moment of quiet.

When Willow finally stands beside him, and finds his glass already empty, her worry grows. She realizes, watching him now, that he's been acting strange since he walked through the front door, and judging by the faraway look in his eyes, it's clear there's something heavy weighing him down.

"Hey?" she calls out, desperate to make him feel better.

He takes a step back when he turns to look at her. The woman he's fantasized about for so long, the woman he's dreamed of building a future with, is standing right before him. Yet now he's not sure if this is what he wants anymore.

"Where has your mind wandered off to?" she asks softly, getting closer to him.

"Willow…" he begins but stops.

"Okay, you're really starting to worry me here, Chase," she whispers, keeping her glass down. She touches his cheeks, but he pulls away, deepening her concern. "What's going on?"

He swallows. "Do you want children?"

"What?" She bites down hard against her lower lips, worried for both of them. "Why are you asking me this?"

He shakes his head, and for a split second, he looks more like a stranger to her. "Just answer the question. Do you see yourself as a mother someday?"

"That's not fair, Chase. That's not a simple question, and neither is the answer. And I think you know that." she says.

"I mean, it's a yes or no answer, Willow."

She says nothing for a while but then changes her mind and leans forward. "Given the current situation, I would beg to differ."

"How so?"

"I could tell you that I see myself as a mother someday. I could say yes, I do want to have children. Or I could be honest and tell you that I've never seen myself in the role of a parent. But I know I want to be with you, Chase. The possibility that you may come with a kid doesn't change that."

Willow shuffles her feet, looking anywhere but at him, because she knows, deep down, everything is changing. Still, she is entirely unaware of the anguish twisting deep inside

Chase's mind because even though she's told him she wants to be with him, it does not ease his anxieties.

I've never seen myself in the role of a parent.

Throughout the week, Chase has been asking himself the same questions about true love and what he really wants. But hearing Willow confess this brings everything back to him—the uncertainty, the fear, the ache, and the pain.

He's tried hard to smother his growing concerns, but as memories of the past flash through his mind, Chase knows it's now or never.

His voice lowers, "How do you know you want to be with me?"

"*What?* Where is this coming from?" She looks him in the eye now and sees the pain settling there.

"A lot can happen to a person in ten years," Chase explains. "Can you honestly say we know each other?"

Willow swallows the lump that's formed in her throat. "I guess not fully."

He nods. "I only know one version of you, and you only know one version of me. Ten years later, we're both different people."

Concern spreads evenly in fine lines on her face. She reaches out for Chase again, but he pulls back a second time, and

Willow starts to fumble for words to say. "But that's what dating is for, no? Getting to know one another?"

"But what is dating without trust?"

Her hand instinctively flies to her cheek like she's just been slapped. His words sting as much. "Okay, what the hell is going on?"

Chase takes a step forward until he's close enough to her. "You claim you want to be with me, no matter what I bring. But how can I trust that you will? How can I trust that you won't leave me again?"

"I promised you that I wouldn't," she says, her eyes brimming with tears. "I *promised*, Chase."

"That was before things got complicated," his hands fly to his hair which he tugs forcefully. His eyes never leave hers, and Willow sees the anger in every fiber of his being.

"Isn't that the whole point of being in a relationship with someone you love?" she asks. "When the going gets tough, you discuss it and work it out."

"This isn't just anything, Willow!" he snaps, his voice raised. "I might be a father!"

"I know that!" Frustrated, she pushes against his chest with her free hand. "Why are you trying to pick a fight with me, Chase? It's like you're looking for any reason to convince yourself this isn't going to work."

He pushes her hand away and replies bitterly, "Maybe I'm just speeding up the inevitable."

"The inevitable?" she asks again because the childishness of the words stomps hard against her heart.

He doesn't stop, and she doubts he will. "The last time I asked you for commitment, you literally *ran* away."

Shit.

Chase regrets his choice of words almost immediately. She flinches when he reaches for her, and a tear rolls down her cheek. He wants to apologize to change the outcome of this situation, but he has no idea what to do or say anymore.

Willow feels betrayal, shame, and anger as the realization hits her. It's been three weeks since she explained exactly why she left him all those years ago, yet here he is, shoving that choice back in her face. Her reasons for leaving all those years ago don't matter to him. Her promise of standing by his side means nothing. The only thing he's choosing to dwell on is that she left.

"You're wrong," she breathes.

Unsure, he says, "Excuse me?"

"The last time you asked me to commit, I promised you I would," she says. "You begged me to stay, and I promised you I would."

"I should go," Chase mutters.

The situation is untenable, and they both know it. Chase doesn't want to be with someone he doesn't trust to stay. Willow knows she can't be in a relationship with someone who doesn't trust her.

"You should," she whispers. "But Chase? Just know, this time, I'm not the one who's choosing to walk away before we can even begin."

18

The Motive Behind Fate

HAS ANYONE EVER DIED from a broken heart, or will I be the first?

It's been two weeks since Chase walked out of Willow's house and, ultimately, her life. Not a single text or call has been exchanged, proof that his outburst was real, that their end was indeed inevitable. What's left is a darkness, an ache that leaves her so empty she fears she may never recover.

Willow glances out of the window as the cab takes her through the bustling streets of Williamsburg. Her sister, Brynn, has invited Willow to stay with her for a few days after receiving a worried phone call from Lina. At first, Willow declined until Lina all but dragged her to the airport.

"You need to get out of this city, Wills," she said. *"Go to New York, see Brynn and Adam, and forget about your life for a few days."*

Willow doesn't want to forget about her life. Despite her deep heartache when thinking about Chase, she wants to remember every detail of that night with him. She doesn't understand where things went wrong; maybe they weren't good in the first place. She wants to believe that every moment they shared was genuine, but the facts don't match. He's betrayed her love, and she resents him for it.

The cab smells strange, so different from the familiar smells of the Chicago taxis. And even though she spent nearly ten years calling this neighborhood home, it feels new to her, as if she's seeing it for the first time. When the car rolls to a stop outside of her sister's home, she climbs out and allows the driver to help her with her bag. She moves it to the front door and glances past her shoulders as the car rolls away, and once again, the loneliness creeps in. The mid-afternoon sun bathes her in a surreal glow, but it does nothing to quell the anger.

The door swings open, and Brynn steps out. Her smile is big and genuine, and it warms Willow's heart.

"Willow Harris, as I live and breathe," she says, smiling. "Get your teeny butt in here!"

"*This* butt is not that teeny," Willow retorts, stepping in and wrapping her sister in a firm hug.

"Yes, it is," Brynn teases. "Welcome to your home away from home, sis."

Willow wasn't planning to visit this soon, but after everything unraveling over the past few weeks, she thinks that maybe Lina was right in pushing her to come. She could use some peace and quiet, away from Chase and brides and everything.

"I can't wait to sleep in my old bed," Willow calls over her shoulder as she pushes the door to her old room open.

"Don't—!" Brynn lunges forward, but it's too late.

"What the hell?" a voice from inside the room calls out.

"Adam?!" Willow blinks, confused. Her brother quickly strides across what used to be her bedroom—now clearly his by the laundry piling up on the chair near the window—and pushes her back out into the hall. "What are you doing here?"

"I live here, dumbass," he responds flatly, crossing his arms and raising a thick eyebrow. "Didn't you used to yell at me for barging into your room? Does this mean I can return the favor?"

"Your room?" Willow turns to look at her twin, "He's sleeping in my room?"

"Yeah, about that...you'll be bunking with me, sis," Brynn responds sheepishly, rubbing the back of her neck. "Adam moved in a few weeks ago."

"And you didn't tell me?"

"I needed a roommate, and he needed a place to crash post-grad," Brynn shrugs. "Besides, you've been a little preoccupied."

"Yeah, with your *boyfriend*," Adam chimes in. Willow freezes, and Brynn's eyes widen. "Where is he, anyway? I half expected him to tag along."

"You didn't tell him?" Willow asks Brynn, her voice shaking.

"Shit, no, I'm sorry,"

"Tell me what?"

"They're not together, Adam," Brynn snaps.

"What?" he doesn't hide his shock. "Already? I thought you two were good together, at least back then."

"They were babies back then, Adam," Brynn snaps bitterly. "People change."

"Come on, B. They reconnect after so long in a random place, that has to be—"

"Stop it!" Willow cries, tears spilling down her cheeks. It makes her both angry and flustered—their back and forth—that it becomes too excruciating to listen any longer. "You're not making this any easier!"

Adam pales, and Brynn's face falls.

"Wills..." Adam tries first.

"Come on," Brynn beckons the siblings to follow her into the house and has them sit on the oversized living room couch.

Willow finds it hard to collect herself as the tears flow freely for the first time in weeks. When she finds herself in her sister's embrace, she gives in to the wrenching heartache, sobbing. It's as if she can't breathe—though she's not sure she wants to, and she doesn't fully understand why.

Adam moves away from the living room to fetch a glass of water for Willow as Brynn slowly rubs her back, softly whispering that everything will be alright.

"This feels worse," Willow manages to state between sobs. "Worse than before. I—I thought that—I thought it would be different this time."

"I know," Brynn's voice is soft.

For a while, silence lingers between them. When falling in love and breaking up, everyone is torn, and there's no mercy in the choice between right and wrong. Still, Adam is the first to break the silence again after placing the glass before his sister. "I'll bury him for you, Wills."

Brynn clicks her tongue and rolls her eyes while Willow releases a blubbering laugh.

Shrugging, Adam continues, "I could. I would, for you. I mean, look at me"—he sits up straight and puffs out his chest—"I'm a man now; I could take him."

"You see the shit I have to put up with, Wills?" Brynn asks, rolling her eyes again. Adam sticks his tongue out and flips her the bird, earning the same response from her in return.

Willow finds comfort in their bickering, a welcome momentary distraction.

Uncertain, Adam leans forward and gently squeezes her shoulders. "Are you okay, though?"

"She's fucking crying, dipshit," Brynn retorts.

"I can see that—"

Willow sniffles, her sobs finally subsiding. In a way, she feels slightly lighter for letting her emotions out and allowing herself to take the first step toward processing everything. "I'm sure I will be, eventually."

"Yes, you will," Brynn states matter-of-factly. "I think this calls for a change in plans for this evening. When was the last time you got absolutely shit-faced?"

"What?" Adam's eyes shoot up. "Brynn—"

But Brynn already knows what he means to say. "It'll get her out of her head for a bit." Then, turning to Willow, "We could stay in and stuff our faces with an unhealthy amount of Pad Thai and wine, or we go out, celebrate that we're all together, and get plastered."

There are times when Willow wonders how she and Brynn came from the same egg; they couldn't be more different, even when they were children. Their mother dressed them in the same outfits until the girls could pick out their clothes, likely hoping they would become mirrored versions of one another, the best of friends. But the only thing Willow and Brynn actually have in common is their DNA.

Still, maybe this level of heartbreak warrants Brynn's way of letting loose. So, Willow agrees, "That could be fun, I guess," she says, wiping away her tears.

Adam stares at Willow like she's grown two heads. He steps back and rubs the back of his neck. "It's your hangover."

But he likes the vibes both ways and wants, above anything, to get his sister to stop thinking about a failed love. In a way, he understands the lines which tie true love and heartache and knows its painful knot.

"Alright, let's get you dressed, sis," Brynn says, standing. "Adam, you gather some bar options."

Adam's chosen option is, he says, the best rooftop bar in the borough, an appraisal with which Willow enthusiastically agrees upon arrival.

Adam makes the first round on him, and when Willow tries to stop him, Brynn holds her back with news. She says, "Carson Design Firm just hired Adam. He can afford it.."

"Carson Design, huh?" Willow toys with the news, allowing it to settle in. To be hired by one of the best architecture firms in the city can only mean one thing. "He's going places."

Brynn leans forward, and her lips curve into a wide smile. "Apparently, Davis Carson has taken quite a liking to him. I bet he makes name partner in five years."

Willow smiles proudly. "And you? Is your name in the hat for any cool new films?"

Brynn shakes her head before she finds the correct answer. Her voice is calm. "An indie thriller I produced was accepted into TIFF."

Willow clasps her hands and lifts herself slightly from the chair with frenzied laughter. "That's amazing, B! I can see it now: *and the award for best film goes to....*"

Brynn agrees, smiling proudly. Producing a hit is something she's always wanted, and getting featured at TIFF will open so many doors for her, but she's taking it slow, not letting herself get carried away as she lets the excitement move through her body in slow and steady patterns she can easily recognize and deal with.

With their drinks set in front of them, Adam raises his glass and leans forward, looking at the sisters. "What should we toast to?"

Willow licks her lips and raises her glass too. "To us being the most creative siblings on the east coast."

"To our reunion!" Brynn says.

And Adam chirps in. "The Harris siblings!"

It's a rare moment of sibling support, something that Willow wouldn't have fathomed years ago. There is something special about befriending your siblings in adulthood. Gone are the days of shouting matches over unimportant things, replaced with bickering that doesn't go too far, banter that only those who've seen you through every stage of life can share. It's remarkable and unlike anything else.

In so many different ways, Willow feels the intensity of the pain, knowing that she'll never fully accept the ending of her relationship with Chase. But for now, she decides to live in the moment, enjoying the company of her siblings and pretending that it doesn't hurt that she's lost the love of her life for a second time.

A while into the evening, Adam gets up and bows slightly. "I'm going to get another."

Willow can tell he's buzzed, but she doesn't try to stop him, finding the sight of her inebriated baby brother amusing.

Brynn smacks her lips and shakes her head, and a lock of hair falls against her face. She does nothing to tuck it out of the way. "Fifty bucks says he doesn't even reach the bar."

Willow raises a brow, then shifts to watch her little brother. Sure enough, not even three strides from the bar, he's approaches a group of young women. "Does this happen a lot?"

"More than you'd think. He has a thing for blondes with blue eyes in particular," Brynn rolls her eyes.

"That doesn't surprise me," Willow laughs. She sits back and crosses her arms over her chest. "Remember that girl he was head over heels with in high school?"

Brynn's eyes widen, and she chuckles, smacking a palm against the table. "Oh, it makes so much sense now!"

"And what about you?" Willow asks, wiggling her eyebrows suggestively. "Are you on the prowl as well?"

"Not in the slightest," Brynn scrunches her nose. She's never been one to date—casually or seriously—preferring her own company. "Do you want to tell me what happened?" she asks, changing the subject. She's always admired Willow's strength; seeing her like this certainly isn't easy because she can see, underneath the façade, the sadness in Willow's eyes.

Willow shakes her head and holds her breath for a while. When she releases it, her eyes are teary, so she tries not to blink, or she'll really cry. Then, the entire story starts to spill out, from the moment they came face to face in the elevator, the late-night conversation in her hotel room, to their reunion after Chase ended his engagement. Willow lays everything out on the table; it feels almost cathartic to talk about it.

"I don't really know what happened if I'm quite honest. Things seemed to be going so well for us. Then, he came over to my place before a dinner date and just started freaking out."

Brynn says nothing, giving Willow space to continue.

"He started by asking if I want kids, and it ended with him telling me he doesn't trust me. He doesn't trust that I won't leave him again. And I really have no clue how I can convince him."

"I don't think there is any way to convince him, Wills," Brynn says, placing her hand over Willow's. "His life has taken such a huge turn in the last while. Two months ago, he was planning a wedding with another woman. You show up out of nowhere, and suddenly everything he thinks he knows changes. I know he was going to end things with his fiancée, but finding out about her affair could not have been easy. The betrayal when a partner breaks trust is not to be taken lightly. You don't get over that very fast."

"I know that," Willow responds, but she isn't sure what she knows or perceives to be right, which confuses and bothers her completely.

Brynn continues, "But despite all that, the universe still wasn't finished with him. I know you believe fate brought you two back together. And I'm not trying to tell you it didn't. But maybe fate brought you two back together for closure."

Willow holds her breath, and a shiver runs down her spine when she hears this because she knows it might be the truth and her clinging onto old memories and what ifs and maybes are just a stall because she can't get over leaving Chase behind again.

"Hard truth, Wills?" Brynn asks, but she doesn't wait for an answer. "You've been hung up on Chase Kennedy for ten years. And when you finally reconnected, it didn't work out. Maybe it's time to let him go. Maybe it's time to start living your life without the *what-if*."

19

You Can't Erase History

CHASE STANDS OUTSIDE HER HOUSE, wondering if he's making the right decision. Perhaps this move is impulsive or dramatic, but he doesn't let that sway him.

The last few weeks have been miserable, so he's giving in to his desires, though now that he's here, it dawns on him that she may not want to see him. She may slam the door in his face, not that he'd blame her.

But the door clicks open just a bit, and she looks at him through the slight space of the partially opened door.

"Chase?" her surprise is real. "What are you doing here?"

"We need to talk," he responds. And when she doesn't budge, he leans in, flashing a cocky smile. "Won't you invite me in, Char? I came all this way."

Reluctantly, Charlotte opens the door all the way, stepping aside to let him in and away from the rain.

Finally, they stand face to face, staring at each other in the fragile silence. Memories flood in of times when everything seemed better, and the idea of 'together forever' made sense, or at least seemed to. But a mutual understanding also settles into the space around them: all that's left between them are these memories—and perhaps a child.

Chase takes in Charlotte's appearance with her signature red lipstick and pearl jewelry; for the most part, she looks the same as she always has, other than the baby bump that's quite pronounced on her small frame. He can't help but stare and wonder if she's carrying his child.

The speech he prepared on the flight over seems unimportant now that she's standing here before him. It's as if seeing her like this—pregnant, glowing, and healthy—has allowed him to let go of some of the anger that's been building up inside him.

Still, he decides to ask the question that needs to be asked in order to move forward.

"How could you freeze me out like that, Char?" he asks and leans forward, and she sees the flash of deep sadness in his eyes. "After everything we've been through?"

She shakes her head, exhaustion coursing through her veins like blood. "Follow me," she says, turning away from him.

Chase pauses, swallowing. "Where?"

"You're right; we need to talk," she replies. "This isn't a conversation for the foyer."

He follows her through the house and into the kitchen. Her arms fly out before her as though communing with an invisible being. Her eyes are on his face, flushed a bright red. "Take a seat, please," she tells him. "I'll put the kettle on."

He sits at the oversized marble island and watches as Charlotte puts the kettle on the stovetop. The action reminds Chase of all the times she would make him tea before she moved back to London. It was something he'd grown accustomed to, and now that it's happening again. He realizes he was looking forward to the resumption of this ritual once she moved back to Chicago after the wedding.

"I don't quite know where to begin," Charlotte breaks the silence with her shaky voice and runs a hand through her hair. Although she's done this countless times in the past, seeing her do this now makes him feel like he's with a stranger.

Chase decides to take the lead. "How's the pregnancy going?"

Giving him a sad smile and instinctively touching the baby bump, she responds, "Pretty well, actually. This one's given me barely any trouble, so I really can't complain."

Chase discovers he'd like nothing more than to know the truth but starts small, knowing that the minor things matter most.

"Have you found out the gender?" he asks.

Her response comes quickly. "We're keeping it a surprise."

We're keeping it a surprise. Oh, it's a surprise alright.

In the end, it means she isn't putting him through the birth of her child, and as her words sink in, indignation laces his quip. The anger begins like a ripple and froth into a storm, and watching her tug at her rolled sleeve, he shakes his head.

"Why would you think keeping this a secret from me was a good idea?"

"Oh please, Chase," her voice is a tangled mess of raised syllables. "Do you really want to drop your entire life for this child? Are you ready to leave your precious firm to relocate here? After all the hours you've spent working towards partner?"

"You're damn straight I am," he hits his hand firmly against the kitchen island and arches an eyebrow. "I'm not a deadbeat, Charlotte Wright. So help me God, if that child has my DNA, I will drop everything to be here for them."

His words destroy Charlotte's picture-perfect dream of having a family with Declan. She and Chase would have to unlearn so much to fit into the co-parenting role; she wants nothing to do with such a process. Swallowing hard, she balls her hands into fists. There's only one move left to make Chase step away for good.

"And what of your future with Willow Harris?" she asks, her manner cool and calculating. "I thought you'd let this go once she came back into your life. Even if you found out about the baby, you would happily accept the out I gave you."

"What do you mean?" The implication of what Charlotte has said strangles his thoughts.

The kettle rings, allowing Charlotte to turn away from his intense gaze.

She prepares the tea as she speaks, her voice low. "Did you think it was a coincidence that I hired her?"

"You knew who she was when you hired her?"

"Of course I did. Didn't Willow tell you?"

"How?" Chase is half aware there is a shimmer of tears threatening to fall but doesn't move to stop them. All he wants are answers.

"I never forgot her name, Chase," she says. "When you told me about her, I knew you would never truly be mine. Of course, I was hopeful, but deep down, I knew."

Chase raises his hands upward and groans. Bringing them down, he tries to shake the pain away. "I was ready to build a life with you, Charlotte. Why would you intentionally bring her back?"

Finally, she turns to face him again. She sets a cup in front of him and looks at him squarely. "For Declan," she responds bluntly.

And then he gets it. Charlotte's plan was to bring Willow back into his life as a tangled web of emotions because she wanted someone else. It breaks his heart, but more than that, it allows him to see the sort of person she really is.

"Declan Williams, Char?" he asks again, and color drains from her cheeks. "That's the other guy?"

Charlotte chews her lip and pulls at her new engagement ring, drawing attention to further proof that she's replaced Chase. He wonders when she received this one. Did she take his off once he left London in favor of the new stone from her new love?

She doesn't meet his eye now. There's sadness and betrayal on his face, and she knows she's the cause. Finally, she whispers, "Yes."

"You told me not to worry about him!" he cries, slapping his palm against the counter hard enough that the tea cups rattle. "You told me you'd moved on!"

She shakes her head, suddenly feeling defensive. "I told you part of me would always love him!"

"As a memory—not a fucking boyfriend! Goddamn it, Charlotte!"

"Chase, listen to yourself!" she says, exasperated. "You don't even see it, do you?"

"See what?"

"The parallels, you idiot!" she cries. "We both got the loves of our lives back, a chance that rarely happens to others. Why can't you just be happy?"

"You manipulated the entire situation, Charlotte!" Frustrated that he even has to explain what he means, her not understanding baffles and infuriates Chase, but he continues. "And for what? To keep your infidelities hidden?"

"No!"

The emotions coursing through him leave him defeated; the frustration and exhaustion wrap themselves around him in an uncomfortable embrace.

"Would it not have been easier, to be honest about your feelings a year ago? You could have stopped this entire mess had you just ended our relationship when you realized you wanted Declan."

"I know that."

"Then why did you do it?" he pushes, struggling to keep his voice even.

"Because I didn't want to hurt you! I didn't want to put you through the same thing she put you through!"

Charlotte's words are enough to shatter the illusion of the Charlotte he thought he'd known and leave him out in the bitter cold of a merciless epiphany. Now, Chase realizes how they've ended up in such a complicated situation. Years ago, he shared the damage Willow had caused him and trusted Charlotte with the reason behind the giant chip on his shoulder. Perhaps it's why they're at a crossroads with no idea where to go or how to return.

She continues, "I know it was wrong to keep dragging our engagement on. If I could go back, I would end things the moment I realized Declan and I still had something. But I can't change the past. When I realized Willow was indeed *your* Willow, I thought the universe was giving me an out. I thought if I hired her, therefore reintroducing you to one another, then—well, fate would do for you what it did for me."

"And the baby?" he asks, shivering—not from his questions or her answers but from the truth preying on his mind. "Did you know you were pregnant when you hired her?"

"Yes. I looked her up as soon as I found out I was pregnant."

"Why?"

She splays her hands at her sides and exhales in frustration. "I thought if she walked back into your life, you would never look back. That you'd break the engagement off and be with her."

Chase says nothing for a long time, but when he looks back at her and speaks again, she hates herself even more.

"I was going to, you know, break the engagement," he whispers. "The day you told me about your affair, I was trying to break up with you. But I wasn't going to end things with you for her. I told myself that morning that I would end things regardless of Willow's feelings for me. Then you admitted to your infidelity, and I knew I'd made the right choice. I just wish it hadn't resulted in losing my trust in you."

Charlotte releases a shaky breath and fidgets with her ring again. "I'm sorry I hurt you."

Stepping around the island, Chase squeezes her shoulders gently. "I'm sorry I made you feel like you would always be second to her."

Charlotte shakes her head to stop him from diving deeper into this unwelcome subject. "I guess what matters is we both ended up with whom we are meant to be with."

"One of us did," he says and drifts away from her. He returns to sit on the chair again and momentarily covers his face with his palm.

She sits beside him and places her hands on the kitchen island. "Aren't you—"

"I left Willow," he says numbly as one merely stating a matter of fact.

"What? Why?"

"I'm going to be a father, Charlotte," he whispers. "How can I trust she'll stick around?"

"You don't know that you're the father, Chase."

"Stop being evasive, Char," he retorts, rolling his eyes.

She sighs. "There's a fifty-fifty chance it's his," she whispers. "More, probably. I've been with him more than I've been with you."

"But we both know where you spent Christmas," his voice is low. "And it wasn't in London."

Looking at her, it feels like the world has fallen apart, and they're alone again. Chase feels so lost, so far away from himself, and as she stares at him, Charlotte blames herself, realizing she feels guilt for making him like this. Chase leans over and trails a finger along her jaw, and she doesn't stop him because, despite what she says, she feels it too.

"We'll always be connected, Char," he whispers, and in an instant, his mouth crushes hers in a heated kiss. He tugs her hair, tilting her chin to meet his waiting lips. Charlotte lets out a startled gasp as though caught off guard, and for a while, she lets him kiss her; she allows herself to get lost in the moment with him.

It takes too long for her to realize the truth behind his hungry kiss: this isn't what he wants. This isn't what either of them wants.

Charlotte pulls away first and wipes her lips with the back of her hand. "Chase, no," she says. "Regardless of paternity, I'm marrying Declan."

Chase moves away from her, hunger replaced by guilt in his eyes. He swallows, realizing the dryness in his throat. "I'm so sorry, Char. I—I don't know why I did that. I don't want this."

"I know," she mutters under her breath.

He shakes his head and runs a quick hand through his hair. She can see the frustration in his eyes and how he carries himself now. "I don't even recognize myself anymore. It's like I've been so lost since…."

She helps him. "Since you walked out on Willow? Did this pregnancy scare her away?"

"Quite the opposite," he says. "It scared me away from her."

"Why?"

"Because it's not just me anymore. When September rolls around, I'm a package deal."

"You don't—"

"Charlotte, I swear to God, if you try to tell me I'm off the hook one more time…"

Charlotte bites her tongue and nods sheepishly.

"And anyway, Willow doesn't even want kids."

"Oh," she responds, touching the pearls around her neck.

Chase releases the breath he'd been holding and pinches the bridge of his nose. This is his weakness: talking about Willow and wanting her with a kind of gentle but animalistic intensity. Her face drowns out his words, and he holds them down for a long time, trying not to forget the lines of freckles on her cheeks and the way her eyes shine with wonder when she comes across something new. He wants her, and even through the deafening pain, she's the only person he wants.

"She tried to tell me that she wants to be with me no matter the child's paternity," he says after a while. Now, back in reality without Willow, his chest hurts again. "But what if the baby gets here, and she realizes dating a single father isn't for her? It's better this way, really. Ending things now saves both of us heartache in the future."

Chase doesn't believe this, but what else can he say? His heart is torn, but perhaps this is for the best.

"Does it, though?" Charlotte asks.

His questioning gaze tells her he wants to know why she's asked this, and she answers. "You're a mess, Chase."

It's not what he's been expecting, but it's close enough because it's how he's felt for a while. "There's just—there's been so much change in such a short time."

Charlotte wants to let him go, but this conversation is something they both need to have. The way he speaks now and the tremor on his lips make her want to sympathize, in as much as she is capable of that act.

"I understand, darling. I do," she says softly. "But you're pushing Willow away when she clearly wants to be here to support you. Even if you are the father, do you really think that'd make her run?"

"It wouldn't be the first time she ran away from commitment," he retorts.

Rubbing the back of her neck, Charlotte grinds her teeth before speaking. "Chase, she was *eighteen*. You asked her for a lifelong commitment when her life was just beginning. There's no way she's the same scared young girl she was a decade ago. Are you the same person you were when you proposed to her?"

He says nothing.

She continues, "I know you're afraid she's going walk out on you again, but Chase, you cannot let that stop you from trying. Fate brought you back to one another; you can't push her away. I have my match in Declan, and you have yours in Willow."

Charlotte says what Chase desperately wants to believe, but the truth is somewhat different. He hurt the woman he loves with all his heart, and now there's no going back.

"I think I've screwed up," he whispers, holding his head in his hands. "I said some really horrible things when I left her."

"I'm sure you can find redemption, Darling," Charlotte responds, gently patting him on the back, talking him down from the mental ledge he's placed himself on. "You know where you're supposed to be. Go to her."

Chase books the last flight out of London after Charlotte promises to stay in touch until they know the child's paternity. He knows he needs Willow as much as he needs the air he breathes. He feels it now, the foolishness of pushing her away again without realizing it, and now a month's passed, and the apology wants to burst out of him, to tear through his lips in a passionate display of ardor and devotion.

In the queue at the gate, he calls her and holds his breath. *What can I tell her? Is she still upset? Will she even want me back?*

"Hi! You've reached Willow Harris! Please leave your name and number, and I'll get back to you."

Willow declines the call, sending Chase straight to voice-mail. He drops the call and slides his phone into his pocket.

It can't be too late, right?

20

Hope in the Morning Fog

THE EARLY MORNING SUN BEGINS to peek over the skyline as Willow jogs along the Gold Coast. She woke up less than an hour earlier with the sudden impulse to run and decided to embrace this urge before it escaped her.

Since her return from New York, Willow has been trying to follow her sister's advice to live life for herself and enjoy every moment of it. The visit with her siblings helped give Willow the encouragement to move on, but Chase's phone call last night left her feeling a little lost.

Why did he call? It's the question she's been asking herself all night. While she's proud of herself for sending him to voicemail, Willow finds herself curious—and maybe a little hurt—about why he didn't leave her a message.

Willow yearned to dial him back when the call ended, but this had felt wrong. Today, she's almost thankful she'd been able to fight the urge because, in some way, it proves that she is ready to start living her life without him by her side. There's something authentically freeing that comes with this realization.

As she jogs down Navy Pier, Willow tries to focus more on her breathing and less on Chase, but both prove difficult, and the air seems to burn in her lungs. She falters and stops, bending over to hold her knees.

"Holy mother—" she groans, feeling, for the first time, cramps in her legs and feet.

"Are you alright?" a deep voice asks beside her.

"Huh?" she asks, cringing, still bent with her hands on her knees.

"Would you like some water?" The question is followed by a water bottle dangling in front of Willow's face. "Are you alright?" the voice repeats, worry evident in its tone.

Willow straightens and sighs deeply. When her eyes meet his, they widen with surprise as though she's seen him before. He chews on his lip, trying to bite back a smirk as he stares down at her, his question hanging in the air. As color returns to her cheeks, he silently offers her the water bottle again, his face twisted in concern.

Her lungs are burning from the strain, so she relents, takes the bottle, and gulps the water quickly. The good Samaritan stands back, trying not to stare.

"Thanks," she says, panting as she returns the bottle to him.

"Are you...new to running?"

Willow rolls her eyes, though she finds his question amusing. "You mean I don't look like a natural to you?"

"Honestly?"

His tone is teasing, but Willow finally looks at him. The first thing she notices about him are his eyes—dark and nearly opaque, two pools of endless oblivion that call to her. As she studies him, Willow realizes just how handsome he is. His entire aura is warm, and although they haven't exchanged many words yet, she finds herself quite taken with the stranger.

"I'm going to die of embarrassment," Willow finally says.

"I've been in the exact place you are," he says holding his smile—his devastatingly beautiful smile. "The key is stretching and hydration."

She nods, keeps her back straight and her eyes focused, the way she's learned to and smiles. "I'll keep that in mind if I decide to do this ever again."

"I hope you will."

Blinking, Willow meets his gaze again. *Huh.*

257

"I just wanted to clear my head," she confesses, though she's unsure why. She continues when he doesn't respond, "It's been a weird few weeks—well, decade, really."

The stranger nods, and Willow wonders if he's encouraging her to elaborate or just being polite.

"I'm Myles," he says when she doesn't continue. "Myles Decker."

"Willow Harris," she replies, stretching out a hand for a handshake. When his large, warm hand envelops hers, she catches her breath. He raises an eyebrow, silently letting her know that, yes, he too feels the spark.

"Are you doing anything tonight, Willow Harris?"

Am I?

Part of her wants to leave and not turn back, to hide under the shadows of her past love but holding back makes her feel even lonelier, and perhaps, this change may be what she needs.

"I am not," comes her response, knowing where this conversation is heading and welcoming it with open arms.

"Would you like to get a drink with me?"

"You work fast," she whispers.

"I just know what I want."

His decisiveness is intoxicating, and Willow begins to question the reality of the moment.

"And what is it that you want?" she hardly recognizes her own voice.

"I want to get to know you."

Perhaps it's sudden, but she finds herself wanting more in their short conversation. So, her answer comes quickly.

"Alright, let's get a drink tonight."

Work normally commands her attention in the same way Myles did, but now... at the office, Willow becomes consumed with wishful thinking: What if she gives him a chance and he makes her forget Chase and the unpleasantness of her failed love?

Willow realizes she very much wants to forget the pain, but also, thinking hard about it; she discovers she doesn't want to forget Chase after a decade of thinking of him and pining for him. Forgetting him feels like a betrayal.

When she tells Lina about Myles over their mid-morning coffee, her friend only has one question: "What about Chase?"

"What about him?"

Sighing, like a schoolmarm dealing with a well liked but not especially bright pupil, Lina approaches the conversation delicately. "What happens if he reaches out?"

"He already did; last night."

"What?!" Lina slams her mug on the table, sloshing the warm coffee across the desk.

"Lina!"

"He calls you after—what? A month?—and you didn't lead with that? Girl, you've been holding out on me!" Lina scolds.

"Well, I didn't take his call," Willow mumbles as she dabs the coffee with a napkin.

Lina blinks, flabbergasted. "Willow…" Her voice trails off, exasperated and utterly at a loss for words.

"Don't say it—"

"Oh, I'll say it! Why the hell didn't you take his call?"

"Because it took him a month to make it!" Willow cries. "I didn't want to talk to him."

And for a while, Lina says nothing. She has the right words now but allows the moment to breathe in the silence, holding back for Willow's sake.

"I've been stuck on Chase Kennedy for ten years. It didn't work out, and it's unhealthy for me to continue pining after him," Willow adds. "I think I'm ready to move on."

"With the *running guy*?" Lina doesn't bother masking the disdain in her voice, her upper curling into the faintest hint of a sneer.

Willow shrugs. "I mean, there's no harm in getting drinks."

"Isn't it a little fast? I mean, it's only been a month, Wills. Also, I can tell you from experience that there *can* be harm in getting drinks," Lina reproves as she grabs a handful of napkins and starts impatiently mopping up the pooled coffee that now seems determined to make its way from the table to the floor.

"It's not like I'm diving headfirst into a relationship with Myles."

Lina studies her for a while. Of course, she understands where her friend's coming from, but part of her is curious if Willow will ever give Chase another chance.

"What about Chase?" she asks again.

"What about him?"

"I just... I think you should call him."

"Why would I?"

"At least hear him out," Lina whispers. "After everything—"

"Lina." The name usually so cheerfully uttered by Willow in affection now becomes a warning.

But Lina pushes on. *Fuck it. If you can be real with your best friend, then what's best friendship for?* "If anything, do it for proper closure. You deserve it; both of you do."

"I'll think about it, alright?" Willow sighs.

"Good."

"But I am getting drinks with Myles," she adds. "He seems like a nice guy, and I'd like to get to know him."

"Fine," Lina says in a tone indicating that this is anything but fine.

Rising to her feet, Willow reaches for her purse. "I should get going if I'm going to meet that new bride for lunch."

It's mere minutes later that the bell to the boutique chimes, alerting Lina of a new arrival. She makes her way to the front and stops short at the sight before her.

Chase Kennedy stands at the entrance, his dark hair a mess atop his head, his eyes wild and frantic.

"Chase?"

"Where is she?" he asks. His voice sounds ragged and tired.

"You just missed her; she's left for a lunch meeting."

"Shit."

"Were you hoping to grovel?" Lina presses, crossing her arms. "Because if you're not planning to grovel, you may as well give up now."

Chase had come straight from the airport, spending the entire ride piecing together an apology and preparing an explanation to make Willow understand that he wants her back. But now, he's at a loss, and all that's left is the rawness of his unspoken words.

"Do you think I still have a chance?" he finally asks, filling the silence.

Lina hesitates, clearly at war with herself.

"I like you, Chase. I do. I believe you and Willow are meant to be together. But you *really* need to get your shit together—no offense," she says, and it feels as though she has so much to say but isn't going to say more. Her eyes bear down against his with such intensity that it startles him.

"It's not offensive; I know you're right," he admits.

"If you really want to be with her, don't give up. Show her what she means to you."

"How?" Chase asks. "Maybe I don't have the right to ask, but do you have any advice, Lina?"

"You're right you don't have the right to ask," she responds bluntly. Then, she sighs, silently apologizing to Willow for what she's about to divulge. "But I think I can help."

"You look remarkable, Willow," Myles says, a warm smile filling his face as they greet one another.

"I'm not underdressed, am I?" She'd spent an hour in front of the large mirror, trying on what felt like a hundred different outfits.

"You're perfect exactly as you are," he responds and leans in, dropping his voice to an intimate whisper as though he's only sharing a secret with her. "Are you looking forward to the evening?"

Nodding, Willow smiles. "I've never been here before. I've been curious to try it out."

"Trying new places and things is what life's all about," he whispers, then holds out an arm. "Right this way, beautiful."

As they walk, Myles's hand brushes against hers, but Willow doesn't flinch—instead, she welcomes the contact. There's a comfortable air between them, and as she settles into it, Willow becomes sure she's walking into a new phase of her life, one that she feels ready to welcome—deciding that she isn't going to worry about Chase or linger in the probability of him still wanting her despite the fact that he knows her far better than anyone else. This time around, she tries to forget him.

Myles leads her into an intimate bar that could pass for a bookstore at first glance. Plush couches and chairs surrounded by bookshelves are in the front, creating a peaceful atmosphere that Willow finds refreshing.

"This way," Myles instructs, a gentle smile plays on his lips.

As they walk deeper into the bar, the atmosphere changes. There are booths lined up against the south wall and tables along the windows, all filled with people.

"Happy hour?" Willow asks, earning a *hm* from Myles.

Distracted by the sea of faces, Willow bumps into a firm chest. "Oh! Sor—"

"Willow?"

She freezes, and her heart leaps into her throat.

This isn't happening. It's a thought—a wish, even a prayer perhaps. But as she's learned, wishes rarely come true, and her track record with prayers hasn't been great either.

"Chase."

"This year," Myles remarks, a pride smile plays on his lip.

As they walk deeper into the bar, the atmosphere changes. There are booths lined up against the south wall and tables along the windows, all filled with people.

"Happy hour?" Willow asks, earning a nod from Myles.

Unnerved by the sea of faces, Willow bumps into a high chair. "Oh! Sorry—"

"Willow!"

She freezes, and her heart leaps into her throat.

This isn't happening. It's a thought—a wish, even, a prayer perhaps. But as she's learned, wishes rarely come true, and her track record with prayers hasn't been great either.

"Chloe."

21

Letting Go of You

WILLOW IS ACUTELY AWARE THAT just behind
Chase, Myles is watching her expectantly. She can see the
curiosity in his eyes, but he makes no effort to interrupt.
It's as if, in his silence, he tells her, *Go. I'll be here.*

"Willow," Chase's rough voice calls out to her. He
gestures toward the entrance, sheepishly asking, "Could
we...?"

She meets Myles's gaze again, who offers her a silent,
gentle nod. Willow wonders if she's so easy to read that
Myles only had to take one look and realize that the reason
for the complicated decade she'd mentioned earlier was
standing between them.

Side-stepping, she allows Chase to lead her past the bustling
crowd and out onto the street. The sun is low, and the sky
is painted in brush strokes of pink and orange. It makes her

think of London when she lost herself in Chase's kiss before he pulled away and admitted that he was spoken for.

When they settle in front of each other, Willow tilts her head back to look at him. He feels taller now, different. His eyes are unrecognizable, and so is the plea she finds in his shaky frame.

Whatever he has to say doesn't matter, she tells herself, but the magnetic pull she's always felt around Chase, the one which ignites her soul, belies this thought, making her stay, making it impossible for her to simply walk away.

They stand in heavy silence, watching one another, wondering who should speak first. Willow figures it's not her turn this time. *Been there, done that.* After all, he's the one who left this time around. So, she continues to wait.

"I didn't handle things between us properly," he finally tells her. It sounds like a recital. But even though his speech is short and stilted, and his movements are awkward, she finds she's still torn by his words and the shared heartbreak they represent. "I felt extremely overwhelmed with everything that's happened in such a short time. And I ran. I was scared that you wouldn't be able to handle all of this—that you'd wake up one day and realize that the life we'd built together is not what you pictured for us."

"I don't know what else I could have done to convince you otherwise," she says, and there's no emotion in her words.

"Nothing," he tells her; it sounds like a plea. "You said and did all the right things. I was just blind. I'm sorry, Willow. I'm so sorry."

Willow's breath becomes shallow as she's suddenly, *violently,* thrown into a whole new life where everything is fleeting, and there's an urgent need for her to adjust to this new life. But, despite her resolution to move on, despite the new man patiently waiting for her to do so, she cannot deny the truth to herself: standing in front of her is the man she's still hopelessly in love with, no matter what. "I wish you would have trusted me, Chase."

He gives her a look, the one which precedes all the love he knows she has, and she melts. "I do trust you now, Willow."

Now. Not when it mattered most.

It's a sad realization, but Willow knows she can't keep up with this anymore. Convinced that she's seen all the signals, the problems they'd tried to bury underneath a mountain of love for one another, and, despite that mountain, she believes their end has truly come this time.

"But you were right, Chase," she murmurs, defeated. "We don't know each other."

"We can start over. Get to know one another again," Chase sounds both foolish and sweet, just the right amount of childishness to make her feel like a young girl again.

Though, she doesn't look him in the eye. She waits, her back straight, eyes on his chest. She takes a deep breath and rearranges her thoughts.

"It's too late," she whispers.

"It's not too late; it doesn't have to be. Not if you don't want it to be." He's pleading again, but it's shot through with a deep desperation this time, as though the thought of leaving things like this might kill him.

There's a pressure Willow feels now that's quite unlike anything she's ever felt, so much more intense than any previous elation of love or desolation of heartbreak. And when Chase closes the distance between them, the pressure spreads from her chest, radiating out to her arms and face.

It makes sense—this belief in a decaying love—but it startles her when he holds her as if he's only holding her for the first time. She flinches, which makes Chase wince and drop his hands. But he doesn't step away from her. He doesn't move from her sight.

"I've been dreaming of you for a decade, but it's time I let you go," she tells him.

"Willow, please..."

Willow holds her pain between her teeth and waits, as she's been doing all this time, for him to say something else, but after a while, she changes her mind. The waiting, she reckons, is the problem. She reaches out and places a hand against his chest. "I need to live my life for myself right now."

A pause. And then, "You know I love you, right?" There is resignation in his voice.

She thinks it's unlikely she'll cry tonight; some other night perhaps, but not this one. But still, it weighs down hard against her chest, this act of watching him, of looking him in the eye.

Nodding, Willow whispers, "I'll *always* love you, Chase."

And there's a slight tremor on his lips when he speaks. "Do you think if we met at another time in our lives, things would have worked out between us?"

"I'd like to think so."

"The timing just wasn't in our favor, I guess," he mutters under his breath, and she feels it—him leaving even though he's still in front of her—breaking her heart.

No. Not breaking. Breaking implies some slight but perhaps repairable damage. More accurately, his leaving *shatters* her heart.

Pressing a slow kiss on her forehead, he takes a mental picture of her pursed lips and the flutter of her lashes because he wants to remember her this way, always. Then, he takes a step backward. "Goodbye, Willow Harris."

She shivers, like one exhausted, but manages to get the words regardless. "Goodbye, Chase Kennedy."

She watches as he walks away from her and the bar he's found her in. He doesn't look back once the entire time.

With him gone, Willow rocks back and forth, inhaling the warm July evening air, trying to control her feelings. A part of her wants to run and find him, to tell him to wait while they try to sort out their feelings, but Willow stops herself, knowing that with him gone, she'll finally be able to move on entirely.

And as if conjured by the mere thought of moving on from Chase, a warm, gentle hand rests on her arm.

Myles.

"He's gone." It's not a question that falls from his lips. Willow nods, numb.

Myles wraps his arms around her, and she welcomes his embrace. Despite only having very recently been introduced, she feels comforted and secure against the warm solidity of his body.

"I know just the place to make you feel alright," Myles says softly, "even if only for tonight."

Willow pulls her head from his chest but doesn't leave his embrace. "Where's that?" she asks, curiosity piqued.

There's a glint of mischief in his eye, a promise of excitement—distraction—which only intrigues Willow more. So, when Myles steps back and offers her his hand, she's more than ready.

She follows him as they half-run through the streets. It only takes a few minutes for them to end up in a dark alleyway. She pauses and looks up at Myles, a question in her gaze.

For a moment, Willow's reminded of the trust she gave to Chase. If it were him leading her here, she would have followed him happily, blindly. *But he wouldn't have done the same.*

"Don't get cold feet now," Myles teases.

"I just realized I've allowed a stranger to lead me into a dark alley."

"Take a leap of faith, Willow."

The invitation is warm, welcoming, and, overall, exciting. Willow's played it safe for so long, protecting her heart; perhaps it's time she did take a leap of faith and depend on someone else for a change.

Silently, Willow loops her arm through Myles's and allows him to lead her to the end of the alley. A staircase, bathed in purple lights, leads to a large oak door that Myles knocks on three times. A slat in the door opens to reveal a man's face and Willow starts.

"Password?"

Beaming, Myles responds confidently, "Marigold."

Marigold.

The door opens, and Myles beckons Willow inside. They walk down a dark hall, and Myles pushes open another large door.

Willow clutches her chest, laughing at the bold manner in which he does this.

"A bar," she says. But it's more than that. A chandelier hangs in the middle, oversized velvet booths line the far wall, and there's a stage with a backdrop of thick, golden velvet curtains near the back of the room. A woman with a strong voice stands in front of a jazz band, belting out a tune. In front of her is a small dance floor filled with couples dressed to the nines.

"Worth the creepy stairwell?" Myles asks, leaning close to her ear so she can hear him over the music.

Willow turns to look at him, blushing. "I feel incredibly underdressed right now."

"My shirt is practically half-open, and I'm wearing a shell necklace, love," Myles brushes a strand of hair away from her face and smiles softly. "You look wonderful."

Willow's cheeks flush, and she bites her lip. Myles takes her hand and nods, "Come on, let's grab a booth."

He leads her across the speakeasy to a cozy corner booth with plush seats. She slides in first, and he scoots in after her. Willow picks up the small drinks menu. "What do they serve?"

"Whatever you'd like, sweetheart," a deep, warm voice chimes in. Willow looks up from the menu to see a short, older woman of, if Willow had to guess, South Asian extraction, possibly Indian, dressed in an eccentric neon-orange jumpsuit. Her graying hair is styled into a sleek ponytail that leaves her large gold hoops on display. She has matching gold bangles on both arms, Willow guesses at least half a dozen. Myles breaks into a warm, brilliant smile.

"I was hoping we'd see you tonight, Marigold!" He slides out of the booth to wrap the woman up in a hug.

"Myles Decker, as I live and breathe!" The woman laughs as he squeezes her tight and pats him on the back, causing her bangles to jingle against one another. "How the hell have you been, kid?" When he releases her, she nods knowingly toward Willow, giving her a sly wink. "Clearly excellent considering your lovely date here."

Willow's cheeks turn crimson when Myles sits down and rests his arm on the back of the booth behind her. "Marigold, this is Willow Harris," he says with more than a touch of pride in his voice. "Willow, this is Marigold Khan; she owns the place."

The weathered woman rolls her eyes and smirks, "As if the name didn't give it away."

"It's a pleasure to meet you, Marigold," Willow greets her warmly.

"And a pleasure to meet you, sweetheart. You've chosen a good dinner companion. Myles here is one of a kind."

"Alright, let's not embarrass me before our night has even begun," Myles interjects and scratches the back of his neck.

Willow laughs. "I'd call that a shining review."

"Yes, well, let's get some drinks, shall we?" Myles pulls the hair tie from his wrist and gathers his locs into a bun. "What can I get you, sweetheart?" Marigold asks, smiling warmly at Willow.

"Would you have an apple gin fizz?"

"Mm! My kind of girl," she winks again and looks at Myles. "Your usual, Myles?"

"Yes, please."

"Back in a jiffy!"

Willow takes in their surroundings for a moment, allowing herself to adjust when she feels Myles's looking at her.

"I'm guessing from Marigold's warm welcome, you're a local?" Willow asks, meeting his gaze.

"When I first moved to the city, a guy I met through work brought me here," Myles replies. "I think Marigold took a liking to me 'cause she invited me back personally." A small smile plays on his lips as he recalls that first meeting nearly a year ago. "The rest is history."

Willow nods, "Is this like a speakeasy?"

"That's exactly what it is. Marigold's grandparents opened it during Prohibition."

"That's awesome!" Willow's eyes sparkle.

"They opened it to be a safe space for all walks of life," he continues. "No matter your race, your sexual orientation, your religion, your wallet size, Marigold's welcomes everyone."

"That's incredible. I would have never known this place even existed," Willow shifts in her seat, and her knees brush against him, the contact not unwelcome by either of them. "Thank you for showing me, Myles."

Myles smiles and puts his hand on her knee. "Stick with me, love; you'll find a lot of what I'll show you will change your life."

There's no doubt that it will.

As the night draws on, and her face is suffused with warmth from the delicious gin fizzes Marigold keeps serving, Myles pulls her onto the dance floor. She's laughing as he spins her around the dance floor, pulling her close, his strong arms wrapping around her.

As they dance the night way well into dawn, Willow imagines what they could look like—her and Myles. Could they be happy together? Or does the lingering presence of Chase in her heart mean any future with Myles is doomed? If she does let him in, if she does take this step forward, will she truly move on? Or will they have their own inevitable expiration date?

Ultimately, Willow decides there has to be a reason they've met. No matter the reason, she feels this is the start of something incredible.

As their time together moves from occasional evening drinks to weekly dinners and eventually three-night-long sleepovers, she begins to forget Chase. As they grow increasingly inseparable, it's only a matter of time before Willow dares to admit to herself that she's fallen for Myles.

22

The Fading Memory of Us

THE WEEKS MELT INTO ONE another as the heartbreak of losing Willow begins to fade into a distant memory, a lingering presence that will likely be around for the rest of his life. His schedule is busy enough to keep him distracted most days, and when it's not, Beck is there to offer him dinner or an extra ticket to a Blackhawks game, like tonight.

"Thanks for inviting me," Chase says as the Uber pulls up to the front of his complex. He flashes a sheepish smile to Beck's boyfriend, Tyson. "And thanks for letting me crash date night—again."

Tyson scoffs good-naturedly, dismissing Chase's apologies with a wave of his hand. "It's no big deal, man."

Chase knows that it's not—Beck wouldn't invite him if Tyson weren't comfortable with it—but he still can't help feeling a little guilty.

"Well, you'll have Beck to yourself tomorrow, I promise. I've got a client dinner."

"Let me know how that goes," Beck says as Chase opens the door and exits the car.

Walking into his dark condo, he kicks off his shoes and tosses his coat onto the ottoman before shuffling to the kitchen. He grabs a bottle of beer from the fridge before digging around for the opener he threw into the junk drawer yesterday. As the beer hits his tongue, he finally allows himself to think about her.

Chase tries not to think about Willow too much anymore; he doesn't want to look back after the progress he's been making. But occasionally, he pictures her when he's alone in the quiet of the evening after a late night out. Sometimes, he hopes that she's miserable without him. But most of the time, he just wishes for her happiness. And tonight, he's wishing for her happiness as a faint, rueful smile moves across his face.

This bittersweet moment of reflection is abruptly cut short by the loud ring of his phone. When he answers, Chase finds himself reeling again. It isn't for Willow. This time around, it's not about her.

It's Charlotte's father, Bart. "It's Charlotte, son," Bart says at the end of the line, and his voice is pained but lowered, almost as though he's trying a little too hard to hide his fear. "There's been an accident."

Bart is the first person Chase meets when he enters the hospital's waiting room. Charlotte's father looks like he's aged ten years since the last time they met, and while this difference is alarming, it's the thought of Charlotte that weighs him down. When Bart opens his arms in welcome he stops thinking and fully sinks into the man's warm embrace, allowing himself to be comforted and to give comfort. Deep down, he knows there's nothing he can say or do that'll console this man, but he wraps his arms firmly around him anyway, trying to absorb as much of Bart's pain as he can.

"How was the flight, son?" Bart asks when Chase lets him go, refusing to let even tragedy shake loose the banalities of polite conversation. Chase shakes his head; he doesn't want to deal with the small talk. Bart seems to understand and says, "Come with me."

Bart takes him to a private room where Grace, Charlotte's mother, is pacing as she clutches a wad of well-worn tissues. Even though they're his ex-in-laws, there is, and always has been, a connection between them that nothing can break.

When Grace sees him, she hugs him, and he holds his breath, thinking if he lets it go, he'll break down in tears. It's interesting, he finds himself thinking, the way priorities change during a crisis.

When she releases him, Chase notices the red rings around her puffy, swollen eyes. Much like Bart, Grace also looks like she's aged several years overnight. She's wearing a thin cardigan and checked pants, her signature pearls hanging gently from her neck, swaying with the rhythm of barely contained sobs. For a moment, he can hear Char whispering in his ear, *She'll be wearing those pearls on her deathbed.* And he responds, *Like mother, like daughter.*

"What happened?" Chase finally gets the chance to ask, tired of not knowing.

"A delivery van hit the town car. She was on her way to the house for the...ceremony," Bart swallows. Grace sobs into her tissues.

"And...the baby?" Chase holds his breath, panic tightly wound in his chest.

"He was delivered in an emergency cesarean shortly after Charlotte arrived at the hospital."

He. A boy.

"Is he...?" Chase asks, not allowing himself to assume the worst.

"Declan is with him now in the NICU." Grace gives Chase's arm a gentle squeeze and sighs. "The doctors have been monitoring him; he's in good hands, Chase."

He nods, his throat feeling thick. Glancing at Bart, he asks a silent question; *Who's the father?*

Bart weighs his options and settles for the truth. "They took DNA from Declan yesterday; we should know within the week."

"Okay, okay. And Char—" Chase swallows, glancing at the curtain separating them from her. "Is she—"

"Oh, God—" Grace sobs again, gripping Bart's shoulders and burying her face against his chest. Bart's gaze glazes over, and something in the air shifts, and among the vulnerability, Chase finds his answer: she's not going to make it. Suddenly, the past, the deception, the cheating means absolutely nothing now in the face of such quiet, unspeakable, grief. As his eyes pass between Charlotte's parents, he perfectly understands their unarticulated expression of love and loss.

He slowly slips past the curtain to where Charlotte lies. Her auburn hair is laid out neatly across the pillows in thick curls, which Chase knows is Grace's doing. It's as if she's asleep, save for the machines all around her, humming and beeping a mournful lullaby in the sad thick fog of impending bereavement. He feels numb and empty. It's mainly because of everything they've gone through together, the bond of shared experience that nothing can break. Having to say his goodbyes for real this time breaks his heart.

"Why don't you take a moment alone with her, Chase?" Bart says, peeking in from the other side before leading his wife out of the room.

When the door closes with a soft 'click,' leaving him alone with Charlotte, Chase begins to cry uncontrollably. As the sobs tear out of him in waves, he feels his heart caving in.

"I'm not really sure how to say goodbye to you, Char," he says between tears. "Not this way, at least."

He longs to hold onto the image of her as she once was: happy, unburdened, and loud. But watching her fade further and further away makes him want to scream at the top of his lungs.

"I want you to know that I forgive you," he whispers, lifting her hand to his lips. "I don't think I could ever hold a grudge, Char, not against you. The truth is, you've changed my life—more than once. You taught me how to love again five years ago. Our time together is something that I will always be grateful for."

As he speaks these words, knowing she will never hear them except perhaps in the next life, assuming there is one, he vows to be the best father he can be if the child is indeed his.

There's a soft knock at the door before Declan enters, standing on the other side of the bed. He offers Chase a sad, tired smile and says, "We should know tomorrow about the paternity."

Seeing Declan again, under these circumstances, feels like an out-of-body experience. Chase studies him closely as if seeing him for the first time and notices the ruffled scrubs and dark circles beneath his eyes. He's worn out, and the grief of watching the love of his life slip away is palpable, hanging heavy in the air.

"Would you like a moment with her?" Chase asks gently.

"I've said my goodbye," Declan whispers, and his voice cracks as tears pool in his eyes.

Instead of marrying her, Declan is losing her for good, and this realization tears Chase in two. What is there to say when you are in a situation like this? Of course, he doesn't resent Declan, but he's at a loss for words.

But Declan doesn't seem to mind silent company, so Chase decides to stay and sit by the window as Declan sits next to the bed; his eyes never leave Charlotte. Chase wonders if he's committing her face to memory the same way he committed Willow's to his own weeks ago.

It's late into the night when Charlotte's parents enter her room, silently signaling that the time has come. Chase holds his breath. The doctor takes off her life support, and in a few minutes, she'll truly be gone, but he waits, hoping and praying for a miracle, anything to keep it from ending like this. The sound of her heart rate flat lining fills the room, and Chase sighs deeply, feeling as though he's exhaled his very soul. The room is silent for a few moments before the doctor calls the time of death, and Declan falls to his knees with a guttural, choked sob.

When grief comes, the detritus of the present life, made up of the many little things that are normally so urgent and important, falls away, leaving one floating where only the what-ifs of the unrealized past and the possibilities of the never-to-be future, become visible. Chase goes through the process without thinking; it is not a process that can be *thought* only *felt*, only experienced. Two days later, as he and Declan sit in the obstetrician's office, he does nothing.

"This is a little unusual, Declan," the doctor argues as he stares at both men. Then, turning to Declan, he says, "Are you sure you wouldn't prefer we discuss this alone?"

Declan shakes his head. "If he doesn't have my DNA, he'll have Chase's."

"Very well," the doctor mumbles and shuffles his papers. "Declan, I'm sorry to inform you that you are not this baby's father."

Silence fills the room as reality begins to sink in for Chase and Declan. For Chase, there's the realization that he is, despite himself, overjoyed to hear this news. It's as if he was too afraid to allow himself to want this when the possibility of it not being a reality hung over his head like a dark cloud.

But for Declan, it's another loss he has to grieve.

Chase puts his hand on Declan's shoulder, gently squeezing it until he meets his eye. Being the father, having a piece of Charlotte to hold on to was all Declan wanted. It's evident in his gaze that his heart has broken another tenfold.

"Do you want to come see him with me?" Chase whispers.

"Really?"

"I haven't met him yet. It would be good to be introduced through a familiar face."

Declan runs a hand through his hair and nods. It's a small consolation, but the truth is Chase knows he's not ready to do this alone, and Declan isn't ready to say goodbye to the child he already loves like his own.

At the NICU, Declan introduces Chase to the nurse as the baby's father, and Chase leans forward to remember this moment.

"Congratulations, Mr. Kennedy," the nurse says. "We're monitoring your son very closely. I'll send in Dr. Zhao to give you the information. He's in good hands here, sir."

"Thank you," is all Chase can say in a hushed whisper before the baby is placed in his arms. He laughs nervously and looks up at Declan. "He's so small."

"He's growing a little bit each day." Declan smiles softly, brushing his thumb against the baby's cheek.

"How long does he have to stay here?"

"Likely until his actual due date," Declan tells him. "He's not fully developed yet, so he needs to be monitored closely."

The baby's face is scrunched up as he sleeps. As Chase holds the tiny bundle wrapped in white, he thinks of his mother and how she'd described what premature babies looked like. He's never really seen one in person until now. His skin has a purplish tint, and Chase can see fine black hair on top of his head.

"Do you know what you're going to name him?" Declan asks, and Chase is immediately pulled back because he has no idea of what name he'll give his son. It's not something he's allowed himself to think about until now.

"Did you and Char have a name picked out for him?" he chooses to ask instead.

"Oliver Noel," Declan says.

"Oliver Noel…" Chase repeats, turning it over in his head. "It's perfect."

It takes Declan by surprise, though. "You want to name him Oliver?"

"That's the name Charlotte chose for him," Chase says. "I think it's a good way to honor her memory, right?"

"Yeah, I do. Thank you, Chase," Declan says. "I know that you have every right to hate me. The way Charlotte and I started up again wasn't right. I want you to know that I'm sorry. But I'm never going to be sorry for being with her. Charlotte's the love of my life. She always was. I won't apologize for that. But you're a good guy. And you deserved better than for us to sneak around behind your back."

"I'm glad Charlotte had you, Declan," Chase says.

Later, after Declan leaves and Chase is once again left alone with the baby, surrounded by nothing but the hum of monitors, doubt creeps in. Now that he knows for sure he's the father, it makes him feel as vulnerable and helpless as his premature son.

Can I be a father? He thinks, watching the baby sleep. Even if he is ready to be a father, he isn't prepared for the reality of becoming a father three months early, and now he doesn't know what to do for sure.

"I'll do my best, Oliver," he says to his son. "I promise."

Chase takes out his phone, dials her number, and his voice chokes up when she takes the call. "Mom? It's Chase."

As the days wear on, Declan begins to visit regularly. His presence makes Chase feel less overwhelmed, so the pair start forming a friendship prompted by the grief of shared loss and the birth of a son they both thought of as theirs.

Chase's mother, Jill, flies in the day before the memorial and keeps an eye on her son as he keeps an eye on her grandson. As a NICU doctor as well as his mother, her presence here gives both a sense of comfortable assuredness and a warm familiarity to Chase.

"You should go home," she urges gently. She sees this a lot when a parent concerns themselves with their baby's well-being and, in the process, disregards theirs.

He shakes his head, declining the offer. "No, I want to be with my son."

"I'll be here," she presses, nudging him away. "Get some proper rest—and a shower, too."

"Do I smell that bad?" he asks, his cheeks flushed.

"Terrible," she says, wrinkling her nose and squeezing his shoulders gently. "I'll be right here when you return, I promise."

But Chase hesitates, glancing at his sleeping son. Swallowing, he looks up at his mother again. "How bad is it, Mom?" His voice is broken, cracking with the fear that only parents know.

There's a moment of hesitation: Jill glances quickly toward Oliver's chart at the end of the incubator and then back at her son's pleading gaze. It's fast, but Chase catches it and urges her again. "Just tell me...*please*."

"It doesn't look great, honey," she whispers. "In all honesty, the likelihood of Oliver making it to his due date is slim."

"How long?" Chase asks, holding back the tears that have sprung to his eyes. "How long do we have?"

"We'll be lucky for a few more days."

For the first time since he was a small child, Chase finds himself breaking down in his mother's arms. She gently wraps him in her arms, softly shushing him as his body rocks with sobbing. He cries into her shoulder, asking her 'why' over and over again, but she doesn't respond. Chase doesn't want the answer anyway; he just doesn't know what else to say.

Against his mother's better judgment, Chase doesn't actively try to leave the hospital. He only steps out of the room when

Declan shows up to check in on Oliver. But today, when he sits outside the NICU, nursing another terrible cup of coffee, he feels the change in the air. Something is happening, and it's happening with a vengeance.

A flurry of nurses rush past him with strained voices. When the door opens, he can hear his mother's distinct shrill yell, the one that she only uses in anger…or in an emergency.

"Do something, goddamnit!"

Chase jumps out of his chair so violently that it falls to the floor rattling in the wake of his departure as he rushes into the room. There's a crowd around Oliver's incubator, and as he approaches, he notices it's empty. "What's going on?"

"Chase!" his mother calls, and he turns toward her. She and Declan stand off to the side, wearing matching expressions.

Time slows, crystalizing into a singularly terrible, endless moment as Chase pushes through the group. The doctor holds the securely swaddled Oliver, his face solemn when he meets Chase's gaze.

"I'm sorry, Mr. Kennedy," he mumbles.

Sorry? For what? Chase reaches for Oliver, pulling him from Dr. Zhao's grasp.

"There was nothing they could do, Chase," his mother interjects, but her voice is muffled. Chase hears everyone very distantly as though they're all underwater. Everyone around him melts away in a blur as Chase brushes his thumb against his son's pale, bluish face.

"Hey buddy, it's Dad. I'm here," Chase coos, "Wake up, Oliver. Wake up." A sob rips through him. "*Please wake up, Oliver.*"

23

The Father

THREE WEEKS LATER, Chase flies back to Chicago without his son.

24

Sometimes Forever Isn't Yours

"WHAT ARE YOU DOING HERE, WILLOW?"

Willow adjusts her footing, glancing around the large hall outside the condo. "Jill called my mom."

"Of course she did," Chase mumbles. Sighing, he opens the door, allowing Willow to pass the threshold.

Inside his home, she feels uneasy. When her mom first called with the news, all she thought of was Chase, meeting and helping him. But now that she's in front of him, Willow realizes she's helpless.

Chase looks like a mess. His face is sporting a generous five o'clock shadow, and his DePaul University sweatshirt is rumpled. Her heart breaks as her gaze meets his. The playful spark that once lit up his eyes is gone, replaced with opaquely dark hollow pools from which no light emanates.

"Chase…" She lifts her hand to reach for his arm but stops short—unsure if touching him will do more harm than good.

"Why did you come here?" he snaps, and she bites down hard on her lower lip at the cold tone of his voice. "Answer me, Willow."

"Of course, I'd come, Chase; you really think I wouldn't?" She's shocked he'd think otherwise. When Chase merely stares at her blank-faced and mute, she continues, "I heard what happened in London. Jill mentioned you haven't left your house since you came home. I wanted to make sure you were okay."

"I told her not to call you," he grumbles.

"To be fair, she didn't call me. She called my mom." Her response earns her a cold glare, and she shivers. Without thinking, she closes the space between them. "Chase…"

"Don't, Willow," and there's a tremor on his lips. "Please just…don't."

"I want to be here for you."

He swallows. Her eyes follow his Adam's apple. "Are you seeing that guy? The one from a few months ago?"

Willow chews on her lower lip before nodding. "Yes."

"Then why come over here?" he asks, exasperated.

"I told you, I want—"

"You want to be here for me, I know. I appreciate it, Willow, but I can't accept your support. Not now. I'm not—I'm not ready for it, okay? I lost my *son*, Willow, don't you get it?" Chase's voice breaks, and with it, his steely resolve. "I still love you, you know? But you said it yourself; you need to live your life for yourself right now. And so do I. I'm trying to process this loss. And honestly, I'm not in a place where I can handle being around you. I need to be alone, I need to grieve, and I need to accept what's happened."

Willow holds her breath as Chase runs a hand through his tousled hair.

"And if I rely on you now, you would only be an emotional crutch. It wouldn't be fair to you, it wouldn't be fair to the guy you're seeing," he pauses, collecting himself, "and it certainly would not be fair to me."

"I understand, Chase," she swallows and steps away from him. "I'm sorry I came here."

Chase nods but says nothing. What more could he say? Willow knows she shouldn't have come here; she feels guilty. So, she steps toward the door but pauses before grasping the handle.

"You know, if you ever want to reach out to me, you can."

"Thank you, Willow."

"Take care of yourself, Chase."

"You too, Sweets."

This will be the last time, Chase thinks. He knows Willow's never going to come back again, and perhaps he deserves this loneliness, this grief, and this pain.

Five years later...

"You've done an amazing job, Kennedy," June proclaims. "I can't thank you enough!"

Chase maintains his professionalism with his client, but he smiles at her when she stretches out a hand and happily takes it. "It's always a pleasure to work with you, June. I'm honored you trusted me with the merger."

June's voice curls into laughter. "You better let me treat you to a drink tonight to celebrate the success."

"Sure," Chase responds instantly, "that would be great."

"Alright, I need to get going," she says. "I'll see you tonight, Kennedy. You better dress up!"

After she leaves, Beck meets him and mimics her in the only way he can. "She's so cute, don't you think, 'Kennedy?'"

"June and I are just friends, Beck," Chase retorts, smiling. "Sometimes I worry about how dense you are, my friend."

"Rude," Beck says, but he's laughing too.

"Will Tyson be making an appearance tonight?" Chase asks.

"Of course he is," says Beck. "He's actually meeting me here right away. We're getting lunch. You want to join us?"

"I'll take a raincheck this time," Chase says, grimacing apologetically. As much as he loves Beck and Tyson, he's spent a little too much time as their third wheel lately.

In any case, he still has a lot to do to finalize June's deal before he heads to London this weekend for Oliver's memorial birthday dinner at Declan's.

Oliver's memorial dinner is a yearly event, something his mother had suggested they celebrate when his first birthday approached. It's a way to honor both Oliver and Charlotte. Now, he and Declan take turns alternating as hosts. It's a lot of traveling, but Chase likes being in London; he feels closer to Oliver when he's there.

Before Beck can respond, Chase spots Tyson enter the firm's lobby and waves him over before heading to his office for the rest of the afternoon. "Enjoy your lunch. I'll see you later!"

Miles away, Willow spends the rest of her afternoon packing the last four years into cardboard boxes. She feels melancholy, though she's not sure why. She'd agreed quickly and enthusiastically when Myles asked her to relocate to San Diego with him. After all, he'd stayed in Chicago for her. In a way, Willow felt obligated to agree, though Myles never pressured her.

As she wraps their dishware in a paper, she remembers how insistent Myles had been that he paid for the movers, but Willow's stubborn antics stopped him. For her, packing is another way of becoming closer to her body and mind, reinforcing the memories she never wants to forget.

But now, as she finishes putting the life she's built with Myles into boxes, Willow's unable to convince herself that she's making the right decision. In the privacy of the apartment she's called home for so long, it's become decidedly more difficult to distinguish the boundary between right and wrong.

Still, she doesn't let herself dwell too much on these lingering doubts. "It's time," she proclaims, clasping her wrists and admiring her handiwork. "I'm ready for this."

Perhaps if I say it enough, it'll actually be true.

Only an hour later, Myles FaceTime's her, Willow's just stepped out of the shower. She wraps the fluffy white towel tightly around her chest before answering.

"Wow, my God, love. You've gotta warn a guy if that's how you answer the phone!" Myles teases, his grin wide and his eyes sparkling.

Willow laughs and sets the phone on the dresser so she can do a little twirl for him. "Satisfied?"

"*Very*," Myles responds. "I wish I wasn't two thousand miles away right now. But thankfully, you'll be here within the week!"

"Yeah," her voice unenthused. Quickly, she asks, "How are things out there? What are you doing?"

"I'm looking at your future boutique! The one you sent me on Monday. Here, look," Myles adjusts the camera and pans over the room he's in. The store is dull, a mixture of beige and white throughout, but she thought it made a great blank canvas. Myles's face fills the screen again, beaming. "I was thinking, once you're settled in at the house, we can take a weekend to paint it however you want. What do you think?"

I should be excited about this. Why am I not excited about this?

Dread washes over Willow as she looks around their nearly empty apartment. Can she really leave this place, this city, that she's called home for so long? Is this the right choice?

I should tell him how I'm feeling. He would want me to tell him. But out loud, she says, "I can't wait! Can you ask the realtor to send me the lease agreement? I'll look over it tomorrow."

"You've got it, love," Myles replies. "Has Lina been by yet?"

"No, she's going to meet me there. I asked her to be there to help with the client." With her impending departure, Willow plans to leave the Chicago boutique in Lina's capable hands, and tonight will be her first solo prep with their longtime client, Zara. "I'm in full guest mode tonight."

"How are you feeling?"

"If there's anyone in this world that I trust with this, it's Lina."

"But how are you feeling about leaving?" Myles pushes. It makes Willow's stomach flutters. He's learned so much about her in the last five years. Sometimes it's as if he can see right through her.

"It's going to be a big change," Willow manages. "But, as you always say, trying new places and things is what life's all about."

"The only constant in life is change," he adds playfully.

"Exactly," Willow responds, smiling while her heart aches. "I should get ready, Myles."

"Of course! I hope you have a great time tonight, love."

"Thanks."

"I love you, miss you, and can't wait to see you!"

After Myles hangs up, Willow thinks back to the new shop again. She'll have to paint it something eccentric to make it hers, then devise a campaign to celebrate the opening of a new location.

It all begins to feel more and more like a burden the longer she thinks it through, and suddenly her chest starts to feel tight. Perhaps it's just too much happening at once, but the unease overtakes her completely.

Rushing to sit on her bed, she bends forward, putting her head between her knees, willing herself to steady her breathing. *What the hell is going on with me?*

Chase sits upright in his chair and groans, running his hands through his hair. This time of year, he always feels reflective. He's promised himself he wouldn't give in to the sadness this time, but there are days, like today, when the pain carries on relentlessly. Chase finds himself thinking about the life he never had a chance to experience.

Today marks what would have been his son's fifth birthday, and as he sits, lost in between worlds, the betrayal of what-ifs comes to mind. If Oliver had survived, what type of boy would he be? What kind of interests would he have at his age? Would he have a favorite color? What would his favorite animal be? Would he enjoy reading? Or playing sports? Or music? Would he be a joyful kid? Would he look like a carbon copy of one of his parents, or would he look like the perfect mix of them both?

Would Oliver feel loved by Chase?

In truth, Chase doesn't know and has no answers to give in response, but he holds on to these questions deep within his heart.

Beck and Tyson are waiting for Chase when he arrives at the Art Institute of Chicago. Beck gives a low, appreciative whistle when he takes in Chase's deep burgundy suit. "Who knew you cleaned up so well?"

"When June tells you to dress up, you dress up," Chase responds, chuckling.

Together, they stroll into the cultural ballroom, and soft music hits Chase. Beck immediately passes him a champagne flute from a passing tray.

"Did you two color coordinate, or is your relationship not there yet?" Beck asks. Tyson chuckles and adjusts his floral tie, which has the same pattern as Beck's suit jacket.

Chase rolls his eyes. "She's a client and a friend, Beck. Nothing more."

But Beck doesn't look like he will back down anytime soon, so Chase excuses himself and goes to find June. It's not hard to spot her in the crowd, especially with her arm linked to someone else's.

"Kennedy," she says when she sees him approach. "You look handsome tonight. You remember Zara, my wife."

"It's great to see you again, Chase!" Zara beams. Her smile is infectious.

"Zara, you look wonderful, as always," Chase says, taking in her emerald green gown. "June is a lucky woman."

"That I am," June chimes in, blushing.

"What, this old thing?" Zara laughs. "It was a gift from June, actually. A custom design, too. She likes to spoil me when business is good, and thanks to you, it's better than ever."

"Well, I'm happy to help anytime," Chase responds.

"I should introduce you to the designer," Zara exclaims. "I think you'd really like her!"

"Oh, I'm actually not—"

"Lina! Come over here!" Zara waves someone over as June mouths *sorry*.

But Chase is frozen to the spot when he catches sight of the woman Zara's waving over. Zara's Lina is Willow's Lina.

He wonders if Lina's expression mirrors his own because she's gone pale, as though she's seen a ghost.

"What are you doing here?" she finally asks, shaking her head.

"Do you two know each other?" Zara asks, confused.

"We've met. Years ago," Lina responds, her tone careful. Chase is rooted to the spot, unable to vocalize anything.

Zara and June exchange glances, shifting uncomfortably in the awkward silence. Until June chimes in, "Well, why don't we leave you two to get reacquainted? We've got some guests to attend to."

The two women take their leave before Chase or Lina can say anything.

For a few moments, Lina's eyes search Chase's. "What are you doing here?" she asks again.

"June's my client—I helped with the merger." Chase shakes his head. His throat feels thick. Another tray of champagne passes nearby, and he switches his empty glass for a full one.

Lina follows suit, throwing hers back quickly. She wipes the corner of her mouth with her thumb before blurting out, "She's going to be here tonight. Willow."

Immediately, Chase scans the room. His heart is beating so fast and loud it's drowning out the soft music filling the room.

"She's not here yet," Lina quickly adds, watching his frantic reaction. "She's on her way."

"Is she…" he doesn't know how to ask.

"She's coming alone."

It has been a long time since Chase heard Willow's name. Hearing it now, it's as if something's awakened in him that he's kept dormant for far too long. He had never reached out to her over the last five years, no matter how much he had longed to at times.

"I—uh, I gotta go," Chase says, moving away.

"Don't!" Lina grasps his arm, and he pauses, his eyes wide. "I mean, don't you—don't you want to see her?"

Chase frees himself from her hold and shakes his head. "It was nice seeing you, Lina. I hope you're well." Then, he makes a beeline for the lobby.

The truth of the matter is simple. Willow Harris loved Chase Kennedy in a way she's never been able to love another. And while she loves Myles, it's not the same.

Willow and Chase shared a love they both felt would last forever. But the thing about forever is it's never guaranteed.

Sometimes, forever isn't yours.

As Chase's heart beats rapidly in his chest, he thinks about Willow again, of her wide-eyed gaze watching him with such curiosity and love, of her soft voice as she shared secrets that she'd never shared with anyone else.

As the elevator slows, Chase steps back and holds his breath. Five years have passed since he let Willow walk out of his life for good. The timing wasn't right for them back then, *but what about now?*

The elevator doors slide open, and he steps into the lobby to wait.

After five long years, he spots her again, hair first—he notices she's grown it out past her shoulders—and then her eyes as she casts them down to the floor. And as she steps toward the elevator, he follows her and links his fingers to hers.

Willow pauses, startled, and glances down at the warm hand on hers. She gasps as the all-too-familiar scent fills her nose, and time stops when she looks up at him.

"Chase?"

"Willow," he whispers.

Acknowledgments

I always see these starting with something like, '*It takes a village,*' I didn't realize just how true that was until I decided I wanted to publish *Forever Yours*—as a 'book-book.' Thank you to my dear friend Josh for holding my hand through every step of the publishing process. You took me behind the curtains to a show I'd only ever watched from the audience—way up in the nosebleeds—and turned me into an author.

To my wonderful editor, Jeffery Howe, who took this on with such enthusiasm and support, and whose presence brought me calm during what I thought would be a stressful process. You took the time to get to know Willow and Chase and helped shape and refine their story into something I'm sincerely proud of. Thank you for your patience, your kindness, and your expertise.

Thank you to Arina Herman and Gene Levi Chan, the skilled artists who took my meticulous vision board-turned-folder and brought it to life. The art you create together is always beautiful, but this one really takes the cake. Arina and I have collaborated on several projects over the years of our friendship, and it was only fitting that we collaborated on my first novel, too.

To the sister of my soul, Lina Wesson, who is the inspiration behind Lina Rose and, much like her namesake, has been the biggest fan of Willow and Chase since the moment I texted her, *'What do you think about this?'* Thank you for loving them and seeing them as I do. Thank you for sitting on Skype with me for hours, working through different scenes. Thank you for adding the brilliant little "London Eye" as the scene breaks and formatting the book to ensure it had the *'perfect final touches.'* I love you and then some.

And to the love of my life, Chez. There are pieces of us in everything I write. You are the reason why I love *love*. And ours? That is forever.

Afterword

I would LOVE to know what you thought of *Forever Yours*!
You can write a review with your thoughts at:

- Amazon
- Goodreads